AWAKEN

LINDSAY PAIGE

LINDSAY PAIGE

First edition: August 2020
Library of Congress Cataloging-in-Publication Data

Paige, Lindsay
Awaken (a The Hourglass Duet novel) – 1st ed
ISBN: 978-1-7325874-6-5

ACKNOWLEDGMENTS

A huge thanks goes to my beta readers, Kristalyn Thornock and Angie Michels Wells. Y'all are always so helpful and help me put out the best book I can!

Thank you to my wonderful editor, Shannon Page, who makes edits a nice process and for doing such a great job!

I must thank Robin from Wicked By Design for having as much excitement over this cover as I did! You brought to life the idea I had in mind, and I could not be happier about the end result! Thank you so much!

There are two readers I need to thank! Naming characters can be a tedious process and both Rometta (who helped me name Chloe's sister, Marie) and Teresa Christianson (who helped me name Isaiah's brother, Jeremiah) pulled through for me when I asked for help. Thank you both so much!

Lastly, I want to thank the readers in Lindsay's League. When I was deciding what to write next, they gave me their input. Some voted for another book that is coming in the future. One voted for this one and another said to follow my heart, which led me here as well. Y'all have always been so supportive and willing to wait for me to push the next book out. Y'all keep me moving and writing on the hardest days. You do more than you realize! Thank you so much!

1

CHLOE

"I don't know if this is working out for us."

My head snaps over to my boyfriend, Cody. He could not have just uttered those words to me. We've been together since I was seventeen. Five years later and he tells me that?

"Why?" I whisper. "What's wrong with us?"

"Are you happy, Chloe?"

I shudder at him using my name. "Yes, of course." I'm not unhappy. I'd much rather be with him than without him.

"I'm not."

He might as well have hit me. I don't understand.

"Chloe, I want someone more independent. Someone more vocal about their wants and needs." He goes on and on, hitting me with nails straight to my heart. He hits on all my weak points, all the things I struggle with, but try little by little to improve on. "We can still be friends. I care about you too much to just let you go. I just don't see a future for us; you don't even know what you want to do, other than what your parents want for you."

Those words, every single one of them, they slice into my heart and release a fury I've never known. I'm sick and tired of his bullshit and all of life's bullshit. I grab the closest object, which happens to be a vase, and throw it near his head. "Fuck you!" The curse that bursts from my mouth startles me. I didn't know I had it in me to say that and I almost want to apologize. How insane is that? He's breaking up with me and I want to tell him I'm sorry for cursing at him.

"Chloe," Cody begins, actually looking hurt and upset, which makes me feel worse and pissed at the same time.

"Stop calling me that!" He never calls me by my name. I'm babe. I've always been babe. Hearing my name on his lips makes me want to vomit. This is his way of distancing himself from me.

"I try, Cody. I try so damn hard and it gets me nowhere. Now you want to break up with me over it?" The resolve in his eyes terrifies me. I stoop to a level I never thought I would, only because I love him so much. "I can try harder. I'll do better. I want to." That's the honest truth. It'll be good for not only us, but for me too. The things he's asking for are things I need to improve on regardless of whether we're together or not.

I can just never make any progress.

He cups my face. "You've been trying for years, Chloe, and you've gotten nowhere."

His words strike harder than me thinking them to myself. They light a furious fire within me. He's giving up on us. I can see it.

"So that's it? We're done because you're not willing to fight for us?"

"I've been fighting since day one!" he argues. "You're the one willing to let life walk all over you and pass you by."

Cody takes a deep breath and releases it as a sigh. "I've graduated and we haven't even talked about where we might go from here. You keep avoiding it. You seem perfectly okay with things as they are. I'm ready to move forward."

He has me there. I'm not ready yet. There is still so much to figure out, to overcome.

Something inside of me breaks completely. It simply snaps. I can't deal with this right now. Not with what's going on with my grandfather.

"If you want to walk away, then walk and don't look back." Where this steely voice and resolve is coming from, I'm not sure. My heart is screaming bloody murder at me. My brain has checked out, refusing to listen. With bated breath, I wait to see if he'll fulfill my heart's desire and change his mind or listen to my brain and walk away.

He nods curtly. When he stands and starts packing what few items he had here, I can't bear to watch. I slide down underneath the covers of my bed and pull them over my head. I can't see him leave. Hearing it and knowing it's happening is bad enough. It's taking everything I have not to toss the covers aside, apologize profusely when I'm not even sure what I did wrong, and promise I'll get my life together. I'll do whatever he wants me to do. But I'm not strong enough to add more to this conflict.

"I still love you," he says a minute later. His voice is low, solemn, and so very sad.

I snort. How can Cody love me and break up with me?

When I stay silent, he finally walks out on me. The moment the door closes, my heart shatters and I can't help but whisper, "I love you too."

The silent tears turn into loud sobs. My heart feels as if someone just died. I didn't know this could hurt that much. How is this possible? Why is this happening to us? How does a person cope with losing the love of her life? The person who apparently doesn't care enough to stay and fight, to stay and figure things out? Everything about this is bullshit. We were supposed to have a great night and it's ended in disaster.

"Chloe? Honey, what's wrong?"

"He's gone," I cry in response to my mom. "For good," I can't help but add. Shoving the covers off my face, I sit up and look at her. "I don't know how to handle this. I don't want to handle this. I need time to rewind. He was the one, Mom."

She sits on the edge of my bed and pulls me into a hug. "You're young, Chloe. If he's foolish enough to let you go, then he most certainly is not the one. You'll recover from this. It'll just take time."

Time I don't want to endure.

"I didn't like him anyway," she adds. Of course she didn't. "Plus, you need to focus on your schoolwork." She forces a smile.

My phone lights up and an automatic smile appears. My grandfather wants to videochat. Thank goodness he's saving us both from the tension that always exists between me and my parents. Mom wordlessly leaves because she knows I'd rather talk to him.

Before I can say a word of hello, my grandfather frowns. "Sweet girl, what is wrong?"

"My boyfriend broke up with me."

"Oh, Chloe. He wasn't good enough for you anyway. You'll be on your way here soon, too. Do you want to talk about what happened?"

I shake my head. "I wish I could come now."

He chuckles. "You're leaving in two weeks. Be patient. I

can't wait to see you. We'll go camping when you get here; I know you want to do that."

It feels like it's been so long since I've visited my grandparents, but it's only been two years. And that's two years too long. My grandpa definitely knows me well. I also like that we're focusing on something other than my heartache.

"I'd love to do that, but will you be well enough?"

He's been in and out of the hospital for a month now. His heart is weak, giving him trouble. He's scheduled for bypass surgery tomorrow, so he's already at the hospital. Grandpa smiles from his hospital bed.

"I'll be fine. I'll be through surgery and out of this damn hospital before you know it. I wouldn't miss doing one of our famous camping trips for anything." He looks at something off screen and I hear my grandma's voice in the background. "Grandma says we've been talking too long and that I need rest. I'll talk to you tomorrow, sweet girl. You don't worry about that boy; he wasn't good enough for you," he reminds me again.

Except he was. He treated me so well.

"Okay," I say anyway. "I love you and Grandma. Tell her to keep me updated."

"She will. We love you too."

The chat ends and I desperately wish I could be in Lupine Grove, North Carolina with him right now. I want to be there when he goes into surgery and when he wakes up, but I'm stuck in Oregon for two more weeks. Between that and the breakup, I make my way outside instead.

Like most nights around this time, I'm lying in the center of our old trampoline, a treasure that I won't let my parents throw away, with my arms stretched out to make my body form a T as I'm staring at the never-ending sky. The soft summer breeze skirts along my legs with more bite than it should have for this time of year. For as long as I can remember, I've been staring at this sky. I've seen all the shades from the pretty, the doleful, to the downright ruthless. It's a sight like tonight that's my favorite. Almost as if the night wonderland knew just what I was seeking when I climbed up here, an old metal spring pinching my leg along the way.

Perfectly centered, the stark white moon hovers above me, daring me to look away. And I do, but only to admire its counterparts. With surrounding hazy but sheer clouds and the constant glimmer of stars dotting the heavens in just the right spots, my view becomes barely complete. Just as the thought occurs, the missing piece ever so casually flies through the air, a blinking light marking its journey. A bleakness travels through my heart, darkening everything as it passes. The same hope I always get when I'm out here whispers in my ear. That taunting desire that sweeps through me every night, singing seductively, begging for me to act, gripping me passionately.

Fly away. Coast through the clouds and never look back. Flee across the country and land in Lupine Grove, the small town where my grandparents live.

My eyes prickle and sting with the unshed tears. It's always been like this and I wish my dad could talk my mom into moving there. While, he's not originally from North Carolina, Mom is. For some reason, she's against moving back. So, I'm left observing the sky every night, watching airplanes, and wishing I could fly away. There's always been an insatiable urge telling me that something is out there, patiently waiting for me to make that one move to set forth the events leading me...to where? Home is the only thing I can think of, and it's utterly ridiculous since I am home. This has always been home.

It doesn't stop that ache which forms within me every single night, pleading with me to be spontaneous. To just leave right this second and drive to the airport. I've pictured the act countless times. A simple smile to the lady behind the counter and I would glance at the schedule one last time. When she asks me which flight I need, my strong and clear voice would utter Jacksonville, the city closest to Lupine Grove with an airport.

But I never do it.

The courage never builds to a level that will shove me over the cliff to send me falling directly to the place I need to land. My parents think I'm crazy. Especially during the winter when I'll grab some blankets just to keep me warm while I gaze at the mocking sky. At eleven p.m., no matter the weather, I'm out here watching. Waiting for something to happen that will signal me to make that move and leave.

I would even have a place to stay because my grandparents still live there. My saving grace is that my parents are paying for my trip, so I can spend two weeks there before I suffer through the rest of summer here. I can't freaking wait until the two weeks here are over. I love Lupine Grove so much.

About as much as I love lying on this trampoline. The view is mesmerizing. The moon doesn't always shine with the same intensity of brightness or shade with the same level of darkness. The stars don't seem to be in the same place, same sequence, and they don't always gleam the same way. Planes don't all fly the same route at the same times. All those things never repeatedly occur simultaneously as one sky.

The finely crafted masterpiece makes me endure such emotions. Surveying the skies isn't just something I do because I enjoy it. It's an incessant craving that I must do in order to find answers. I don't know what I'm looking for, what I've always been looking for, but I know that it's here on this ratty trampoline that I will discover it.

Hours later, I watch a lone aircraft glide from one corner of my view to the other. I send up silent positive thoughts for my grandpa's surgery and I doze off.

AWE FILLS me as I absorb my surroundings. I'm standing on what appears to be a solid cloud, looking at the sight just over the edge. Ah, I love it here already. It smells like fresh rain is about to fall. I love the smell of an impending storm and that lovely aroma is overwhelming here. And the view! It's the view I'm always wanting to see. Lights scattering the city below act as stars from up here. Buildings are mere shapes clustered together. It's breathtaking and haunting. A misty fog settles feet from the ground and makes a thin blanket.

"Sweet girl?"

Whirling around, I find the source of a familiar voice, which seems to hold a touch of apprehension.

"Grandpa?" I rush over to hug him fiercely. I've missed him so much.

He's dressed like normal, jeans and a button-up plaid shirt. As usual, the scent of shaving cream that always seems to follow him around fills my nose as we embrace. When I pull away, I notice there's another person standing next to him. The guy's not but an inch taller than me, but he seems to tower over me with a huskiness that oozes power and strength.

"There's someone I want you to meet," Grandpa says with a smile at the man, who is dressed in only dark blue jeans. I try not to get distracted by his body that is molded by his jeans, his bare feet shifting his weight nervously. "This is Isaiah and he needs you."

"What are you talking about?" I ask, confused, even as I shake the man's outstretched hand. "Who is he?" Almost positive I've never met him before.

Grandpa laughs heartily. "I just told you, sweet girl. This is Isaiah. He needs you, so stay here with him. I've got to go." Grandpa pulls me into another tight hug. I close my eyes, loving his comfort and missing him even more. "I love you, Chloe. Always know that."

When I open my eyes, my arms are empty and Grandpa is gone before I can ask what he means. Isaiah is still here, though.

"Isaiah?" I ask, unsure why I'm questioning his identity.

He nods. "Do you like this view of the city?" He's Southern, like my grandparents. His accent is heavy and prominent.

"I love it." The response slips from my mouth without a second thought as I turn to face the gorgeous view once more. "It's what I've always dreamed."

"I'm glad you like it." Isaiah walks over to stand next to me, stuffing his hands into his pockets. We glance at one another at the same time. It's then I realize how piercing and intense his sharp hazel eyes are and how dark his short black hair is. His freckles appear to be delicately placed along his nose and cheeks, just as the stars are aligned in the sky. "Chloe," he begins, but everything suddenly disappears as droplets of water begin to fall.

I LUNGE UPRIGHT, the dream quickly forgotten. Lightning strikes off in the distance and the misty drizzle turns into a torrent of unrelenting rain with a roar of thunder. We haven't had a storm like this in forever! Fumbling my way off the trampoline, I dash into the house. The storm continues to rage as I run to my room upstairs using the back staircase. It didn't take me more than forty-five seconds to run inside but that was all it took for my clothes to stick to me like my own skin. A chill seeps into my bones. I shiver as droplets of water fall from my hair and run down my back. I peel off my shirt and toss it in the hamper, followed by the rest of my clothes.

Yanking open the second drawer of my dresser, I find a pair of pajamas and get dressed. I settle into my bed with wishful thinking of flying away and drift into a slumber.

"CHLOE, WAKE UP." My mother's sad voice awakens me as she shakes my shoulder.

I open my eyes as I stretch, but stop in mid-movement upon seeing her red eyes and tear-streaked cheeks with my father standing next to her. My stomach and heart drop. No. No. No. I'm scared to ask, but do anyway. "What's wrong?"

Mom moves to sit on the edge of the bed, a loud creak matching her movements. Her voice trembles and more tears fall as she says, "Grandpa died this morning."

No. The tears quickly fall as a sob clutches my chest. The pain is immense as so many questions fly through my head. What happened? How is the world supposed to keep turning without Grandpa? I don't want to be awake right now. Mom wraps me tight in a hug. I'm not sure how long we sit there, crying, but my tears don't seem to stop. This can't be real. I'm still dreaming. I must be. The world would never be so cruel as to take away my grandpa, to take him away from me and my grandma. My sadness feels like a dark wave, as dark as the darkest night. It crashes over me and consumes; it swallows me whole.

When Mom pulls away, she says, "We're catching a flight out this afternoon, so we need to pack." She wipes my cheeks with her hands, but I barely notice because I feel so numb. This has to be a mistake. My grandpa was the most supportive person in my life; he can't be gone! Part of me thinks to text Cody, but I quickly dismiss that idea.

My parents leave to pack and my eyes shoot over to the picture on my nightstand as I lie back down. It's one of my grandparents and me. We're smiling and happy; we took it the last time I was with him. This is a nightmare, right? I was supposed to go see him and we were going camping. A fresh wave of tears hits me as I slowly force myself out of bed to start packing. Poor Grandma. She's all alone now. What is she going to do? I was only going to spend two weeks with them, but now, I wonder if I could stay the entire summer. There's nowhere else I'd rather be than as close to Grandpa as I can be, even if he's not here anymore.

Leaving my suitcase open on the bed, I walk down the hall toward my parents' room. Dad is doing the packing while Mom sits on the edge of the bed and watches with a vacant look in her eyes.

"Mom?"

She lifts her head. "What is it, Chloe?"

"Can I stay with Grandma until I have to start school in the fall?" Part of me doesn't know why I'm asking for permission. I'm twenty-two. I shouldn't need their permission, but I'm always seeking their approval. And the news of my grandpa dying has me feeling like a six-year-old again, wanting him to hold me until I feel better.

"Grandma would love that, I'm sure."

"Thanks." I return to my room and begin to pack. I'll

only need a few clothes because my grandparents have a room for me at their house, being their only grandchild who actually visits, and I keep clothes there. Once that's done, I start grabbing the things I'll want with me while I'm there. My laptop and a handful of books.

With my hands propped on my hips, I feel accomplished as I stare at my luggage.

"Don't forget something for the funeral," Dad says, poking his head into my room.

My shoulders sag. Right. The funeral.

"What happened?" I blurt out.

Dad steps into the room and sits in the chair at my desk. "There were fatal complications with his surgery," he says with a sigh.

Fatal. The word is like a punch to the gut, knocking the air out of my lungs. My lip quivers with the tears wanting to fall again. "But he said he would be fine," I say, my voice squeaking. He promised he would be okay.

Dad comes over and hugs me. The tears unleash, wreaking havoc on Dad's shirt. I cry until my eyes can't manage any more tears. Dad keeps pushing Mom and me to do this and that to prepare for our flight. On and off, I debate whether I should call Cody. It would be nice to share my remorse with him. He has met my grandfather and would want to hear this news as well.

But he walked away.

He didn't see a future with me. Maybe we should make it a clean cut. All day, I open and close our text messages, preparing to reach out, but then I think better of it. The day seems to pass in a blur. Once we're on the plane, I finally feel more at ease, if only because we're headed to North Carolina. It doesn't take long before I fall asleep.

"You're back."

The relief pouring through his lips is overwhelming as I pivot to face him. I've returned to that cloud-like place above the earth and he's standing a foot from me. It's as if time hasn't passed at all. Easily, he closes the space between us. His fingers twitch. He folds his arms over his chest and rocks slightly on his heels.

I remember the last time I was here and it feels like mere seconds ago. Only this time, I feel different. More aware. I know I'm in a dream. I know who I am and I sort of know this man, right?

"Who are you?" I ask, just in case.

A soft smile flashes and he says confidently, "My name is Isaiah, remember?"

Yes, Isaiah. Isaiah with the deeply Southern accent. Grandpa said he needed me. "Where's my grandpa?"

The smile slowly disappears, his eyes are so telling, and I remember getting the news this morning of his passing. "I'm so sorry for your loss," Isaiah tells me.

Here, the tears refuse to fall. "How did you know?"

"I heard," he says simply. He tilts his head and begins walking toward a bench I'm sure wasn't there a second ago. Not knowing what else to do, I follow him. We take a seat. Isaiah seems tense. His arms are still crossed over his chest. He leans back against the bench and one of his legs rocks back and forth as if it's a nervous habit.

"Why did Grandpa say that you needed me?" I ask.

Isaiah glances down and shrugs. "Because he's a smart man. I've been close to giving up and he thinks you can be my reason to hang on."

My brows pull together. "I don't understand."

"I don't either. All I know is he thinks we'll be good for one another." Isaiah scoffs. "Sounds ridiculous, but there's not much I can do right now." Isaiah sighs. He stares at me for a moment and then says, "You'll see me soon, Chloe."

Isaiah begins to fade and I panic. "Wait!" To my surprise, he becomes completely tangible once more. I know because I reach out and run my hands over his strong, muscular, warm upper body to ensure that he is indeed here. I don't know why, but I can't stand the thought of him leaving. "Don't go. Can't you stay, Isaiah?"

A knowing and sad smile appears slowly. "I can stay a bit longer, but you must sleep."

I don't want to sleep. But when the bench beneath us transforms into a bed, Isaiah closes his eyes as if he's going to sleep too. A heavy drowsiness suddenly falls over me. To keep from falling asleep, I decide to question him.

"Do you like Ferris wheels, Isaiah?"

"I don't hate them."

"Are you going to leave again?" I ask. The concern is disturbing with its power.

Isaiah doesn't answer my question like I'm expecting. Instead, he says with the utmost confidence, "We'll always find each other, Chloe."

I STARTLE AWAKE with our descent. The vividness of the dream sticks with me in an oddly comforting way. Why am I having weird dreams? I shake my head as if it could rid me of the lingering comfort it seems to have brought. Right now, I need to focus on Grandma.

IT'S ALMOST NOON. I didn't wake up until an hour ago and then I had to shower and get dressed. It took me forever to fall asleep last night. Knowing Grandma was in her bed alone and Grandpa wasn't there was hard to swallow in my own room. Eventually, I got up and snuck into their room. Grandma was awake, which surprised me. She patted the spot next to her and let me crawl in. The dam broke. She held me until I fell asleep.

All I want is to hug my grandma except the house seems to be full of people, stopping by constantly to give their condolences. Shouldn't they be giving her more space? That again, this is the South. I eventually find her with my parents and my sister, who drove in as well, in the kitchen. Grandma is always a sight to be seen. With her silver hair and always tastefully done makeup, she still makes sure to dress nicely.

And then there's her pink slippers.

At some point in the last few years, she decided she was done wearing shoes. All she'll wear now is a very worn out pair of pink bedroom slippers. It's adorable to me. My mom hates it. That makes me love them even more.

Her eyes are wet and glassy, but she manages a smile when she sees me. "Hey, sleepy head," she says, holding out her arms.

I step into them, hugging her tightly and trying not to cry. There's too many people in her small kitchen. And so much food covering every inch of her counters; no wonder it smells so good down here. When I pull away, she grabs the car keys from a basket on the counter.

"Will you do me a favor?"

"Of course."

"I forgot his tablet. Will you go to the hospital and pick it up for me?" I nod because there isn't anything I wouldn't do for my grandma. "Thank you. I'll have a plate of food for you when you get back." She could feed the entire town and half of the next one with all the food she's been given.

Part of me doesn't want to go anywhere near the hospital, while at the same time, I'm anxious to be there. Like seriously anxious. My grandparents live in a small town, but my grandpa spent his final days in the hospital across town instead of the bigger, better one forty minutes away. I feel fairly confident about being able to remember the route to the hospital. It feels good when I actually make it without any problems. It's a small feat, but a feat nonetheless.

I stand outside the large brick building, staring at it. Grandpa died here. Tears begin to fall and I'm lucky I don't sob. What must it have been like for Grandma while she sat, waiting for good news only to get the worst news possible. God, I wish I could've been here at least.

With a deep breath, I hurry inside. Grandpa was on the fifth floor, so I take the elevator up. His tablet is supposed to be waiting at the nurses' desk. There are two ladies sitting in front of computers. They smile when they see me.

"Can I help you?" one of them asks.

I swallow hard. "My grandma left my grandpa's tablet. Daniel Jones," I add his name.

Her eyes sadden. "Ah, yes. I'm sorry for your loss, honey. Just one moment." She stands and disappears into an office behind them. A moment later, she returns with it.

"Thank you."

The tablet feels heavy in my arms as I walk down the hallway toward the elevator. I have his tablet. There is no reason to stay in this hospital. Only, I can't leave yet. This was where he took his last breath, spent his last night, and here was where he last spoke with me. He was in room 538.

My eyes flicker to the nearest room and the number on the plaque.

534.

The next room is 535, and suddenly, my feet are moving until 538 is in front of me.

The door is open. By the soft beeping sounds coming from inside, there's probably already a new patient inside. I wonder how they can stand it here. The antiseptic smell. The eerie quiet that booms down the hallways. The occasional hustle and bustle that makes you fear something bad has happened to someone else and that they might be coming to this room next. It's a horrible place. But the urge to see where I last spoke to my grandfather is overwhelming. Slowly, I step into the room, hoping the patient is alone and sleeping.

I gasp when I see him.

The man from my dreams, Isaiah, is lying in the hospital bed, hooked up to a machine that's breathing for him. How is this possible? I move forward until I'm next to him. He's paler than in my dreams, but that black hair is the same. Those freckles that dot his nose and cheeks are the same.

"Are you a friend of Isaiah's?"

I swivel at a female voice, a nurse. Oh, my God. His name is Isaiah. It's actually him! "Y-y-yes," I stumble. "I just arrived. Just heard he was here." The lies start pouring from my mouth. "No one has told me anything yet. What's wrong with him? What happened?"

Sympathy causes the nurse to frown. "He's in a coma, has been for a month or so. He got hit by car, poor thing. If his body can heal and if nothing gets worse, then we're hoping he'll wake up." She looks over the machines, checking vitals, I guess.

Once she appears to be done, I ask, "Can I have some privacy?"

"Of course."

She disappears into the hallway, and I stare down at the man. He's around my age, I think. Even pale and on a ventilator, I can tell he's handsome.

I don't understand. How can he be real? Am I hallucinating? I slowly reach out toward his hand. Mine hovers for a moment before I lower it. God, he's real. How is this possible? The nearby chair is in its normal spot and I wonder if that means no one has visited. How can someone so young not have visitors? I don't want to let go of his hand, so I gently sit on the edge of his bed.

I place the tablet behind me and then pick up his hand, allowing my fingers to trail over it. This is crazy. But definitely happening. His hand is warm, soft, and a bit larger than mine. It's silly in many ways, but I'm desperate for him to wake up, twitch a finger, something.

"How can I figure this out if you can't talk to me, Isaiah?" I whisper, flicking my eyes between his closed eyelids and his hand.

Nothing happens.

Remembering Isaiah saying he's sorry for my loss in my last dream combined with my confusion brings tears to my eyes. I gently place his hand back onto the bed. Grandma is expecting me back soon and this is too crazy for me to handle.

As I leave the hospital, I know I'll be back to visit Isaiah.

2

CHLOE

"I don't know how to figure this out either," Isaiah says when I see him again.

My eyes widen with surprise. "You heard me?"

He smiles. "Yes. You have a beautiful voice. It's different than here. Never heard someone who didn't have an accent like mine." He glances around us.

We fall into an awkward silence as if meeting for the first time. Isaiah nods toward the bench and we head over wordlessly.

"You sounded sad today."

"I went to my grandpa's funeral."

He nods in understanding.

"Can I ask you something?" I ask and get a quick yes. "Has anyone visited you?"

Isaiah's smile is fake. "You did," he answers.

My heart aches for him; why wouldn't someone visit him? Don't they know about his condition?

"There are some things that cannot be explained right now, Chloe. Like this." He motions to the air around us. "How are we even here? Will you come see me again? Talk to me?"

"What will I say?"

"Anything."

"Okay." I don't know why I say it, but I do.

Isaiah grins. "Thank you. I'm sorry about Daniel," he finishes, turning solemn.

"I'm sorry you're in a coma."

Isaiah shrugs. "My body needs time to heal itself. I'll wake up," he replies confidently. "You should rest. You'll have to wake up soon yourself."

"But I'm asleep now," I say, confused. I had to fall asleep to come to this place.

"Yeah, but you'll be tired the longer we're here. You just will be."

The bench transforms into a bed like it did last time. Isaiah and I lie next to one another, knowing another word won't be spoken today. I don't understand what's happening, but it sure is a welcome distraction.

WHEN I WAKE up that morning, I am slightly tired as Isaiah said I would be. I lie in bed, listening to the sounds of my grandma moving about already. The aroma of food swirls around my nose, teasing and tempting me. There are entirely too many emotions beating inside my chest. With a sigh, I get up. Grandma shouldn't spend her morning alone for too much longer.

Grandma glances over when she hears my footsteps. "Good morning."

"Morning, Grandma."

"I hope you're hungry."

"I am," I lie.

A few minutes later, Grandma sits down with our feast

before us. She isn't that hungry either because we are both slow to eat. But I manage to force some food down because that's what Grandma would want and maybe if I eat, she will too.

My mind wanders to Isaiah. Should I see him again today? He wants to talk, but what would we talk about? How would I explain leaving? Is any of this even real? What if I'm losing it and none of it really happened?

"Is something bothering you, dear?"

I look up from my food to my grandma.

"Do you believe in spirits or ghosts?" I end up asking.

Oddly enough, Grandma smiles. "If you'd asked me that last month, the answer would've been no. But then..." Her eyes water. "The night Grandpa left us to be with the Lord, I was sleeping when it happened." She places a hand over her mouth. Her eyes squeeze closed and a few tears slip out. Once she's regained her composure, she takes a deep breath. "He came to me," she says with wonder in her voice. "We said our goodbyes in this beautiful place I couldn't even begin to describe."

My eyes widen. "He came to you too?"

Grandma blinks. "What?"

"I saw him that night too!" I can't believe it. Well, it doesn't shock me that Grandpa made sure to say goodbye to her, but it does that she a similar experience as I did. "He didn't exactly come and say goodbye, though," I add with a frown. "He wanted to introduce me to someone."

"I'm confused. Who did he introduce you to?"

"Um..." Do I share with her? I've already shared this much. "It's a guy around my age, I think. And it turns out he's in Grandpa's room now, currently in a coma." My brow furrows as I remember what he told me. "He said he needed my help. I'm so confused."

Grandma stuns me when she laughs. "He said you would probably come to me and ask for help with something, but he wouldn't explain what. I had no idea that your grandfather appears to have orchestrated something like this. Tell me exactly what happened."

Feeling relaxed with Grandma's support, I rehash everything. With every word, it's as if I inject life into Grandma. Or as if Grandpa is via me. When I'm done, with our breakfast nowhere near finished, Grandma stands.

"We need to go see this boy." She looks around her kitchen. "But first we must bring him goodies."

I want to point out that he won't be able to eat them, but this is the best I've seen Grandma in a few days. I don't want to rain on her parade. Grandma shuffles around and immediately begins baking. She orders me upstairs to shower and look halfway decent for when we visit Isaiah. Again, I want to point out that he won't be able to see me, but I don't.

After I get myself ready for the day and Grandma has baked goodies, I drive us to the hospital.

"How are you doing since the breakup? Did you tell Cody about your grandfather?"

"No. I'm doing fine."

Grandma sends a glance my way. "I know Grandpa didn't like him, but I know you did, Chloe. You've experienced a lot of loss lately."

That's an understatement. "It's been nice to be here away from Cody. It's made it easier to not think about him." I still find myself thinking of him from time to time, but the craziness of the times has made it easier to try and push my failed relationship out of my mind. My heart aches just thinking of him now.

"He meant a lot to you," she says.

"Of course he did." I just don't think I meant that much

to him at the end of the day. "I don't want to talk about it anymore."

Grandma obliges.

A few minutes later, we arrive at the hospital. But we don't get out right away. The last time my grandma was here, she came with Grandpa, but left without him. We sit in the car in silence for a good fifteen minutes. Tears silently stream down her face before she takes a deep, loud inhale and looks over at me.

"Let's quit piddlin' around and give this boy some much needed company."

With that, we exit the car and make our way inside the hospital. We follow the familiar path to his room. It seems even longer than it did yesterday, our footsteps echoing in every hallway. Grandma hesitates outside of his doorway. I do too, wondering if I should wait with her, or give her some space. She answers my question for me when she nudges me inside with the basket of cookies she baked.

The sight of Isaiah steals my breath away once more. He looks so much more alive than in my dreams, yet at the same time, he looks so...still and lifeless. His features manage to be both vibrant and dull. He somehow looks cold and warm. It's a war that confuses me further.

Still, I walk over to his bed and set the basket on the table next to it.

"Hi," I say softly. "I brought cookies. Hopefully, it's a better smell than what you're used to. And technically, my grandma made them. She's here too. I ended up telling her about you and she wanted to come. I hope you don't mind. It's someone else who can talk to you," I point out as my grandma finally walks completely into the room.

She stands on the opposite side of his bed and holds his hand. "It's nice to meet you, Isaiah. Chloe told me you met my Daniel. For him to want us here with you must mean you're a special young man." I watch her squeeze his hand. "Don't you worry about a thing. You've got the both of us now and we'll make sure you're well taken care of."

Grandma isn't lying either. She presses the call button and immediately startles the nurse who walks in and recognizes her. Grandma ignores it and starts interrogating her. "When was he last checked on? Have you moved him around lately? How is he doing today? You might as well list us as his emergency contact, too. How much longer do you think his body needs to rest?" The questions go on and on without the nurse having a chance to answer any of them.

I chuckle and glance down at Isaiah, wondering what he's thinking about all of this. I lean down and whisper, "You asked for company. Hope you can handle this." With a little laugh, I pull away. The nurse drags Grandma out of the room so she can speak with the doctor as she demanded. I take a seat in the nearby chair and get comfortable.

"I really hope you don't mind me bringing my grandma," I say, "but I ended up telling her about this weird thing with us and it just seemed to give her some purpose. I think she needs that right now." My gaze trails over to the basket of cookies. I reach over and grab a chocolate chip for myself. "Sorry if the smell is making you wish you could really have one. She insisted, and I didn't have the heart to remind her you wouldn't exactly be tasting this right now." I take a bigger bite than I would if Isaiah could see me. "Mmm. This is delicious." It's still warm and soft, too.

Oddly enough, it doesn't feel weird to talk to him like this. I thought it would. I do worry that I may run out of things to say at some point, but for now, I'm glad I can talk to him like he wanted. Grandma returns to the room with a triumphant look.

"I don't think they were looking after him as well as they could have. They will now," she says with confidence. Grandma takes a seat in the other chair and pulls the bag off her shoulder.

"What do you have?" I ask as she pulls out a bundle of something colorful.

"My crochet bag. I've been working on a blanket for your grandfather." She stares at the partially completed blanket. "I guess I'll either have to keep it or give it to you now." She glances at Isaiah. "Or maybe Isaiah would like it."

Grandma leans back in her chair and begins whipping the yarn around the needle and transforming the small movements into more of the blanket. It's interesting and a little fascinating. Apparently, my watching is disturbing her.

"If you're going to be nosy, then you might as well learn. I never could get your mother to learn, so I could pass this skill down. It's well past time that I've taught you how."

As if her bag has no bottom, Grandma pulls out another skein of yarn (something I just now learn that it's called when she hands it to me) and a needle. She tells me to find a pattern on that "handy phone" of mine. From there, as we lean over Isaiah's legs, Grandma shows me how to crochet. She even jokes that when Isaiah wakes up, she'll be teaching him too.

3

ISAIAH

The room has fallen silent. For a moment, I'm not sure if I should panic because that means my company has mysteriously disappeared or if I should enjoy the silence. After another brief second, I decide panic is best. My rooms have been silent, aside from the nurses and doctors, for far too long. Now that I have noise, I crave it.

Although neither woman can tell, I relax upon hearing Chloe harshly exhale. "What am I doing wrong? It keeps getting smaller! I thought you said this would help me relax. I'm probably upsetting Isaiah because this is anything but relaxing, Grandma."

Her grandma only laughs and I feel their presence around my legs. Not exactly a feeling, but a weird sensation that tells me something is near my legs.

"Let me watch and see what you're doing wrong."

Chloe makes another noise. A minute or so later, her grandmother explains something about how she did a stitch wrong. Chloe groans and complains about unraveling all of her hard work. Other than TV, I'd never heard a non-southern accent before I met Chloe. If "met" and "heard" are even the right terms to use. It's interesting to hear something unlike what I'm used to. It's like fresh, much-needed cool rain after a hot, long drought; it feels so good.

I don't really know why I'm doing any of this though. I don't know her. I didn't know her grandfather. It's not like I have many people in my life, even fewer who I trust. It feels nice to have someone around, even if it is a stranger.

"What do you want to do the rest of the week?" her grandma asks after another lull of silence. Chloe doesn't answer right away and I hear the old lady say, "Don't look at me like that, sweet girl. I'm sure Isaiah wouldn't want us cooped up in here with him all day every day."

Yes, I do, Gloria! Ah! Finally! That's what Daniel said her name was! Gloria has no clue what I want; I absolutely, selfishly want them here as much as they can be here without me being even more unreasonable.

"You don't have much time here, Chloe."

Wait, what?

"Grandma!"

Chloe's going to leave?

"Oh, I'm sorry, dear. But we still need to spend time like Grandpa would have wanted."

Where is she going? Back home?

"This is part of what he wanted."

When?

"We're not going to abandon the boy, Chloe, but he can't be our life while you're here."

Why not, Gloria? I've been bored and alone for a long time. Not that I'd ever admit it to anyone, but I want their company. What if I never wake up? What if my brother thinks I completely abandoned him? What about Autumn? She has to be worried sick. My brother and my best friend probably think I'm dead in an alley somewhere. If I'm wrong and I never wake up, I need someone who I can talk to to help me communicate with them when I'm ready. They are all I have. I may not be all they have, but that doesn't mean they can think I'm dead or gone.

"What's going on?" Chloe asks, sounding concerned.

"I don't know. Let me get a nurse in here." Again, I feel a presence up by my arm.

"What if we've upset him? He can hear us, remember?"

Am I reacting in a way that's noticeable? I silence my thoughts and it's then that I hear the heart monitor beeping like crazy. It slowly begins to settle as one of the nurses enters the room. This nurse is one I don't like and of course, she doesn't believe a word from either of them when they tell evil Rita that my heart rate jumped and soared.

Things are quiet for a bit and then Gloria clears her throat. "Are you looking forward to returning to school? It's your last year."

"Yay," Chloe answers in a tone completely devoid of excitement.

"There's always time to change your major, dear."

"Tell that to Mom and Dad," she grumbles.

"Life is too short to go through it being unhappy and not doing something you love."

"I don't want to go through this again, Grandma," Chloe says, sounding so defeated and tired.

I wonder how many times they've had this conversation. Daniel said I had a mission with his granddaughter, but he didn't elaborate on what it was. Maybe I need to convince her to follow her own dreams instead of her parents'. If that's what it takes for me to wake up, then that's exactly what I'll do.

Man, I'm tired. How it's possible that I get tired when I'm

in a coma and have been doing nothing for who knows how long now is beyond me. How a person sleeps when like this is another question I'm not sure how to answer, too. But alas, I can feel myself drifting to sleep with the sounds of Chloe and Gloria whispering about crocheting.

4

CHLOE

Something feels different. I don't know how to explain it, but I feel like Isaiah isn't with us right now. Before, it was almost as if I knew beyond a shadow of a doubt that he was present and listening to us. But now? He seems distant. His body seems stiller. Where did he go? Has something happened? Is he gone for good now? Am I going crazy? Imagining things that don't really exist? How am I to know what's really true or not anymore when things I never thought were possible can apparently be possible?

"Maybe we should go."

Grandma frowns. "After that fit you just threw?"

I shrug. "I don't think he's with us right now."

She tilts her head. "What do you mean?"

"I don't know. Something feels different, though."

She eyes me for a moment before nodding. "Okay, sweet girl. If you want to take a break, we can."

Part of me doesn't want to leave him after that episode with his heart rate, but then again, maybe a break would be nice.

The next few days carry on like this. From morning until noon or so, Grandma and I hang out with Isaiah as I learn the infuriating task of crocheting. After that, we go out on the town, exploring and doing things my grandpa normally did with me. Which means we stopped by the convenience store and learned all the gossip going around town while drinking coffee with other old folks. We grab something to eat from a local hole in the wall restaurant. We stop in the local hardware store to say hello to the owner. Grandpa would always pick something up, but we don't because we wouldn't even know where to start. We return to the hospital for a few hours before returning home for the night. Then, I'd spend my night making small talk with Isaiah again in my sleep.

Things have been a bit weird since my first visit with my grandma. We keep conversation light. Nothing too personal. Slightly flirty. But it seems obvious to me that heavier topics of conversation linger in the back of our minds.

Tonight, when I meet with Isaiah, he is the one who breaks the ice.

"How long are you here for?" he asks.

"Only two months," I reply with the heaviness of that answer in my tone. "I'm supposed to go back for school."

Isaiah nods, turning his head to look out at the skyline. "What's home like? What were you doing before you came here?"

"It's nice. We live in one of the nicer areas of our suburb. Other than getting the news about Grandpa, the last thing that happened was my boyfriend breaking up with me."

He swivels on his feet and pierces me with his stare. "Boyfriend?"

"Ex now. Apparently, I'm a doormat and he only wants to be friends since we're obviously on two different paths." I roll my eyes hard, hating to even say the words.

"What paths would those be?"

I sigh, but I'm also grateful that's the part he's choosing to focus on. "Both of my parents are teachers. Well, my dad just became assistant principal. I think they both want me to do the same since I'm obviously not going to be a doctor like my sister; that's what I'm going to school for at least." I'm still not sure what I want to do. Well, I'm not sure I want to be in the education system like my parents, let me put it that way. "He goes to a different college an hour away from mine to become an IT guy; just graduated actually." Mentioning Cody to Isaiah is weird. Talking about him still makes my heart skip a beat; it just hurts to do it now.

"You don't sound excited about your future."

This is not something I want to talk about. I've talked about it enough with my best friend back home, who I should probably call here soon. To slide right away from that question, I ask, "What does your path look like?"

Isaiah laughs humorlessly. "I don't know if we should talk about mine."

"Why not? We talked about mine."

He sighs. It's the kind of sigh where upon hearing it you realize you're about to get bad news and the other person is not looking forward to sharing it. "There's a lot you don't know about me, Chloe. Once you find out, you might not want to come back, and I actually enjoy your company."

I don't even know that I'm choosing to come here in the first place. Still, I'm all he has right now and I'm not going to abandon him.

Unless he murdered someone. That's not something I can handle.

"I promise I won't go anywhere," I tell him despite his very skeptical look. "I keep my promises, Isaiah."

His gaze finds the skyline before turning back to me. "Why should I trust you?"

"Who else do you have right now?" I point out.

His eyes narrow. "Your grandpa said you could be pushy."

I laugh. "I'm not pushy." I'm the furthest thing from being pushy. "What do you have to lose by telling me?"

Isaiah watches me for a moment and I start to think he won't tell me anything of substance, but then he says, "Three months and six days before my accident I stopped using."

"Stopped using what?" I ask with confusion.

"Cocaine."

Oh.

I've never known anyone who did drugs. My parents have kept me pretty sheltered and put the fear of God into me from as early on as they could when it comes to anything like drugs or alcohol or cigarettes. I can't imagine or relate to anything regarding this experience.

"Disappointed?" he asks, still staring at me. He makes the most eye contact out of anyone I've ever met.

"I just don't know what to think. This is something new for me."

That makes Isaiah laugh. "For some reason, it don't surprise me you're that innocent."

I'm so tempted to correct his grammar, but I think better of it. Instead, I ask, "Why did you do drugs?" There has to be a reason, right? A huge, life-changing reason? People don't just wake up and decide to snort or inject themselves with a deadly drug. Right?

Isaiah shrugs. "The foster care system isn't all rainbows and sprinkles, Chloe. Life afterward isn't much better either." He takes a deep breath and his hands ball into fists. "My life fucking sucked. My parents were dead. My brother hated me because I couldn't save him fast enough. It seemed obvious to me that the best choice was to get hooked on cocaine."

My jaw hangs about an inch from the floor. His parents are dead? He has a brother? Where is he? I'm unable to ask any of these questions before our bench transforms into a bed and Isaiah rests a finger over my lips. Our first real point of contact. Chills run down my entire body as my eyes widen.

"That's enough for tonight, unless you want to tell me why you're going to school for something you don't seem to care about?" He eyes me with a slight smile and raised eyebrows, waiting to see if I'll give in. I won't. He doesn't trust me and I don't trust him, even though I'm asking him to trust me. What a pickle we're in, as Grandma would say. "Get some rest and come see me tomorrow." He searches my eyes. "Please?"

I nod. He gives me a weak smile. I'm grateful he opened up to me even if he's not allowing me to delve into this topic just yet. I stare up at the beautiful sky I love so much. He's very still and stiff. I relax into the bed, wishing I was brave enough to ask more questions even though I know he doesn't want me to. But I'm not brave, so I stay quiet and fall asleep.

WHEN I AWAKEN in the morning, I'm slammed with questions. As nonsensical as it sounds, I'm anxious about getting to the hospital to release some of these questions I have, although I know I won't get any answers in return. I don't even know if I want answers. This is so out of the ordinary for me that I don't know how to wrap my head around it.

I've never met a drug addict before.

If my friends have ever tried drugs, they never told me.

I've never felt so sheltered in my entire life. What were my parents thinking? They kept me away from so many things and now I don't know how to handle this type of situation. What if I'm not strong enough? What if I'm too dumb to handle it? I feel that way right now.

"You seem preoccupied today," Grandma says after I've looked up from my crochet project for only the twentieth time to look at Isaiah and sigh before getting back to what little progress I've been making.

"I learned something new about Isaiah last night in our dream."

Grandma glances between the two of us. "Well? Do you want to tell me or not?"

"He's not alone," I say to start. "He has a younger brother, but he's in foster care still." Grandma transitions her gaze to Isaiah. "He said his parents died and he grew up with foster parents. I don't know much more about that particular tidbit. But he also said his brother hates him—"

"Oh, I doubt that," Grandma interrupts.

"And he's a recovering drug addict."

Her eyes widen. "Well, I declare." She continues to crochet as if I didn't just throw a bomb out there. Her legs are crossed and one foot dances and swings, the pink slipper looking as if it'll fall off at any moment. Grandma glances at Isaiah. "It takes a strong person to come back and fight off the grip addiction can have on you."

Well, I certainly wasn't expecting that. "How do you know?" I blurt out.

Her eyes find mine. "I just know, Chloe. I also know that it helps to have a great support system. The fact that he's doing this on his own is a testament to his strength and determination. And I'm sorry, Isaiah, but I'm not sure how much longer you could go on without some support of some kind. It's good we're here now."

Except I'll have to go home and be miserable at some point.

"How am I supposed to help him? The only thing I know about drugs is you aren't supposed to do them."

Grandma chuckles. "You'll be fine, my sweet girl," is all she says.

I'll be fine? I angrily wrap yarn around my crochet needle and weave it in and out of the stitches. She was no help at all. I lay a bomb like this on her and this is the best she could tell me? I'll be fine? What kind of Grandma do I have anyway?

"Wow. Where did that come from?" I ask in awe as I stare at the massive hourglass that has joined our dreamland.

"I don't know," Isaiah says from next to me. "But it started running the moment I got here."

I glance over at him. "You get here before me?" I figured we both popped in at the same time.

He nods. "About a minute before. I have a bad feelin' about it, Chloe," he replies, steadily watching the sand drop to the bottom. "Maybe when the sand runs out, so does our time here."

"Maybe that's when you'll wake up?" I suggest hopefully. "There's a lot of sand too," I add.

"I don't like this." Isaiah turns and stalks away to the balcony that overlooks the skyline. After one quick glance at the hourglass, I hurry after him. "I heard you tell your grandma about me today."

"Did you not want me to?"

Isaiah takes my hand. "I don't care. My past isn't a secret, whether I'm ashamed of it or not. I brought it up now because I feel like she didn't satisfy you obviously wanting to talk more about it."

Would it be weird to say I like Isaiah? I'm not sure what version or what all encompasses how I like him, but I like him. He's definitely different than what I'm used to. I'm not sure how I feel about this either when part of me misses Cody every day. But Grandpa was right about one thing, too: Isaiah needs my help and I'm determined to help him.

"Why do you think your brother hates you?" This is something that has been bothering me. Does he think this because he hasn't come to visit?

"Ever since I aged out of the system a few years ago—"

"Wait. How old are you?"

Isaiah laughs. "I'm twenty-three."

Oh. "I'm only twenty-two," I squeak. I suddenly feel so much younger than him. Maybe because his life experiences are vastly more developed than mine. And maybe because he only answers to himself while I find myself constantly answering to and trying to please my parents and everyone else around me. "Anyway," I push.

"Anyway, I've been struggling to stay afloat and," he shrugs, folding his arms over his chest and rocking slightly on his heels again. "And then I started doing cocaine, so that didn't help me. But Jeremiah wanted me to get my shit together so I can get him out of the system. He's been pissed since my eighteenth birthday that I haven't gotten him out yet." With every word, his shoulders droop more and more. His words carry a heavier and heavier load. His eyes crinkle and look sadder than a lost puppy.

"After he told me how his foster parents, who I thought were nice, aren't that nice...well, I knew I had to get my shit together once and for all. I wanted to be better before for him, but it just seemed too hard and I thought he'd be better off with them. I quit the cocaine. I got an okay job." Isaiah shakes his head and laughs. "And then I ended up here. I know he's madder than hell right now because he doesn't know where I am."

"He's probably scared," I correct him. "Why don't I go tell him, Isaiah? I can do that for you."

"No," he replies instantly and harshly. "My brother doesn't know you. He won't trust you. You ain't gettin' in the middle of my mess."

"But I can check on him for you," I point out.

"No."

We stand in tense silence for a moment before I remember something else.

"What about your best friend? Don't you want him to know? He could go talk to your brother instead?"

Just when I think I've hooked Isaiah, he shakes his head again. "I'm glad you're here, Chloe, I am, but I don't trust you enough to get you involved."

The ground shakes and lightning strikes, momentarily blinding us. A loud boom has me clutching my ears. Within seconds things are back to normal. My gaze finds Isaiah, but his are glued to the hourglass. There's a crack in the upper bulb and sand is now falling out of it and onto the ground as well.

"Told you it was bad news," he mutters.

"We must be doing something wrong. I'm here to help you. That's what my grandpa said. You're not letting me help."

"Get some rest," he sighs as we fall onto the appearing bed beneath us.

Why is he being so stubborn?

I may have lied to Chloe.

Any time I sleep, or what I call sleeping in a coma, I go to our place. I'm there now and I stare at the huge hourglass. My gut tells me the same thing it told me before I walked into my first foster home: this will not be good.

Why is it here? What is it counting down to? Why is it so big? A little one couldn't have served the same purpose? I run toward it and try to push it over. The damn thing is heavy! I keep pushing and pushing, grunting and groaning, sounding like a dying man, until it starts to tilt more and more. With one final shove, it falls over. I expect a large crash with glass shattering everywhere, but instead, the damn thing disappears just before it is to hit the floor. It reappears in its exact spot, pushing me out of the way, and the sand is exactly as it was.

That seems like an even worse sign.

I scream in frustration, my fingers digging into the inside of my palms. How am I supposed to get out of here when I'm losing so much time by the second?

"I could tell you what it's for."

I whirl around to find Daniel. My heart beats a million times faster at the sight of him.

This seems like a bad sign too. A dead man is in our place? Does that mean I'm dead now too? Or will be soon? Was my gut wrong about me waking up?

"Daniel, please tell me you being here is a good thing."

The old man laughs. "You're not dying, if that's what you're really asking."

Well, that's a relief. I thumb over my shoulder to the stupid hourglass. "What does this mean?"

"You're running out of time."

"For what?"

Daniel shrugs. "I don't get to divulge that much information yet. How's my granddaughter?"

"She'd be mad if she knew I was talkin' to you right now and she wasn't." That makes him laugh. "She's doin' good. So is your wife." He smiles. "I want to wake up so I can really talk to them."

Daniel loses his smile and my stomach drops to the floor. "Not yet."

"When the hourglass runs out?" I ask hopefully.

He shakes his head. "Not then either."

Then what the fuck is it counting down to?

"All I can tell you is make the most of every grain of sand, Isaiah. Use your time here wisely. Trust Chloe," he stresses. "Tell my girls I miss them and I love them." As soon as the last word leaves his mouth, he disappears as suddenly as he appeared. He wasn't any real help at all.

Except that he confirmed that this hourglass is bad news.

6

CHLOE

W here is he? I don't know how I know he isn't here to begin with, but he's not with us.

We've been here for two hours so far and Isaiah hasn't been with us. But as sure as I know it, something in my gut changes. I perk up in my chair.

"Isaiah?" I search his face as if it'll change. "Are you here now? Where are you when you aren't here? It worries me. You definitely need to answer this tonight."

Grandma chuckles and I glare at her.

"It's not funny," I chastise.

"He's a young man who hasn't been anywhere in over a month; you see him during the day, you haunt his dreams, and you're concerned about where he's been. It sounds a little funny, Chloe."

I swear. This woman. "I do not haunt his dreams, Grandma."

She smiles at me. "You need to lighten up, sweet girl. Maybe we need to get out of here and have some fun."

Isaiah just got here. Without thinking, I reach out and grab his hand. "Not yet. We can't leave him yet."

I look at his hand, analyzing it. The bony knuckles. The blue veins popping up as if they want to break through the skin. The hair curled over and seemingly perfectly in place. It's a nice hand. A manly hand. It's bigger than mine, so mine fits nestled perfectly inside.

"Your parents will call you tonight; they are a little concerned you haven't called them."

My attention turns to my grandma. With everything that's been going on, I've honestly forgotten to call them. "Should I tell them about Isaiah?" I ask, already disliking that idea. They wouldn't understand.

"That's up to you." Grandma eyeballs me pretty hard. "How is it going with your folks?"

I shrug. "They think it's a great idea for me to be on the path for education; to follow in their footsteps."

"I never knew that's what you wanted to do," she says, even though she knows that it absolutely is not what I want to do.

"I'm not sure I do," I admit and then hold my breath for her reaction. She may know I'm resistant to my path, but I've never actually said the words aloud.

Grandma rests her yarn and crochet needle in her lap. "Chloe Romanski, no granddaughter of mine will be miserable in a job for all her life. If that isn't what you want to do, start thinking about what you would want to do. You better use your time here wisely, sweet girl."

Half a beat passes before Isaiah's heartbeat steadily climbs before it starts to race once again. As my grandma stands, she says, "Use this time to figure things out without the pressure of your parents hanging over your head." She reaches for the call button and presses it before grabbing Isaiah's hand. "Calm down, boy. She's in good hands and so are you. Everything will be just fine and dandy, won't it?"

"Yeah." What she says sinks in hard and quick. "You really think that maybe I should do something else?" It is as simple as that? I think of something, pick it, and just do it?

"If that's what you want, absolutely."

Isaiah's heartbeat eases back down bit by bit.

"I didn't know I could really pick something else; I don't know what I'd want to do." Everyone, even Cody, has always pushed me toward what they wanted me to do.

A nurse finally comes in just as his heart rate is back to normal. It's the mean nurse. Once she realizes nothing is amiss, she scowls and leaves the room.

"You'll figure it out, sweet girl. We'll all figure it out together."

"I feel as if they will be disappointed no matter what because I'm not like Marie."

Grandma cuts her eyes at me. "Let's not go down that road, Chloe. You are your own person and your parents know that."

ISAIAH IS GRINNING when I see him. "You look like you're about to burst," he says with a little laugh.

"I have questions and things to discuss. First," I hold up one finger, "where do you go?"

"When you think I've left and then come back?"

I nod.

"I'm resting. Sleeping. That's what it feels like, at least."

"Oh. It feels like you're gone. Like gone gone."

Isaiah rocks on his heels, almost unsteadily, and then suddenly pulls me into a hug. "I'm there, I promise. I'm going to wake up, remember? How can I be gone gone when I'm going to wake up?"

Wow. This hug. I love this hug. I need to live in this hug. The comfort oozing from this hug is like nothing I've ever felt before. That's saying a lot considering I thought my grandpa had the best hugs ever. But this? This is a whole 'nother world type of hug. Then again, we are in another world.

But his voice. Isaiah seems uncertain now. Why? Should we be worried?

"Second," I say into his chest, feeling the heat leaving my mouth blast right back onto my face. "Why does your heart keep scaring us?"

He chuckles again and calmly pulls away, reverting back to his usual comfortable stance with his hands in his pockets. "I don't think y'all were scared today."

Well, that's because we're almost certain he's reacting to what we're saying.

"I can hear you, remember?" I nod and he sighs. "Your grandma just said something that startled me a little."

I look up at him, confused. "What do you mean?"

His shoulders drop. "I don't want to tell you this, but maybe it's not a good idea to lie either."

"You think? Lying is never a good idea."

Isaiah only shrugs. "I saw Daniel today."

I suck in a breath and then the air in my lungs stills. "What?" I breathe.

"While I was sleeping. I was furious over that damn hour-glass and I saw him. He said he could tell me what it meant, but all he would tell me is that I need to make the most of my time here. When your grandma said the same thing to you, it just shocked me. That hourglass does mean something bad, Chloe."

The hourglass is meaningless to me right now. Isaiah saw Grandpa. "Did he say anything else? How is he?"

Isaiah smiles. "He seems fine. He said to tell his girls he loves and misses them."

My eyes well with fat tears. "It's hard to be without him."

"I know. But hey. You still have the rest of your family." He pauses and then says, "I have a surprise for us. Close your eyes. I want to try something."

There's not an ounce of hesitation in my body as my eyelids race to close. Excitement courses through my body as I wait for him to tell me when I can open my eyes again.

"One day I want to try taking us somewhere other than here, but I don't want to try that just yet. I can change things here, so..." That's news to me. I hear him take a deep breath and feel the exhale on my forehead. "Open your eyes."

It's as if we're in space almost. The light source has darkened dramatically, but there are seemingly thousands of twinkling lights surrounding us. We're now seated at a table, decorated romantically with candles, roses, and...dinner?

"We can eat here?"

Isaiah shrugs. "Why not? It'll be interesting to see if you actually feel full in the morning," he says with a little smile and a laugh. "I thought we could use a change of pace."

I nod in agreement. We sit in awkward silence for a long moment. "The food looks good," I finally say as I pick up a fork. It looks like we have an array of veggies with duck and some sort of sauce. My senses seem to be in overdrive with the aroma filling my nose. Even the delicious scent of the roses battles the food for power. "Smells good, too." Wonder if I'll really taste it with the smell being so strong?

Isaiah hums in agreement and we take our first bite.

I can totally taste the deliciously spectacular food. "Can you cook?" I ask him.

"Had to learn once I was on my own, but I don't know too terribly much." He keeps his eyes on his plate as he responds. "You?"

"I can make breakfast, but that's about it."

He looks up at me with a crooked smile. "Man, I was hoping you could bake like your grandma."

I laugh. "I'm sure I'll get lessons while I'm here." After taking another bite, I hesitantly ask, "How was it being on your own?"

Isaiah shrugs. "Not too different than being in the system. I just didn't have a place to come home to most of the time. Sometimes, I was able to find someone with a couch I could crash on. Not always the safest of situations, but..." He shrugs again. "But once I got clean, things were better. I was saving up and just got my own apartment. Then this happened."

"What did happen?" It just hit me that the nurse only mentioned a car hit him, but Isaiah and I haven't talked about it.

"I was working a double shift and was walking back home one night." Isaiah laughs, but it's completely devoid of humor. "All I remember is bright lights coming at me and a revving engine when I was crossing the street. I heard the cops talking with the nurses." He shakes his head. "Witnesses leaving a bar said it looked like the person was coming right for me. They saw the whole thing. That's the only reason I didn't die. One of them called 911 and got someone there right away. But they haven't been able to find who did it."

Wow.

"Sad thing is, had I been drunk or high, my injuries might not be as bad because I wouldn't have tensed up. I'd have been too high to react. How fucked up is that?"

"That's horrible, Isaiah." I don't know what else to say. He wishes he was high when it happened.

"It doesn't matter now." He refocuses on me. "If you could pick your career, what would you want to do?"

I groan. "Don't ask me hard questions I don't know the answers to, Isaiah. It's rude."

He laughs and with it, I smile. Can I stay here with him forever? Things are too easy, too perfect, and too nice.

"Fine. Tell me about your family."

I open my mouth and then close it, remembering the way he was the last time we brought up his family. "Why should I tell you? Why should I trust you?" I throw at him, as if I might actually be honest with him. I don't know if the words I sometimes let slip in my head can be spoken aloud. Even here.

Isaiah stares me down with this cold look that makes me want to apologize. "Whether I want to or not, whether it feels natural or not, I'm trying." He waves his arms all around us. "Because that's the only way I'm waking up. If I can try to trust you, you should trust me too."

My head tilts to the left with confusion. "Wait. What do you mean that's the only way you're waking up?"

"When Daniel visited me, he talked about the hourglass." Isaiah takes a moment to glare at it while continuing, "He said to use my time wisely, make the most of every grain of sand, and then he emphasized really heavily that I was to trust you. I have no choice, Chloe."

He sounds as if trusting me would be the worst thing in the world. Or the hardest thing.

Then again, if I were to be completely honest with Isaiah, or with everyone in my family? Yeah, that would be unbelievably hard to do. Maybe I could start with Isaiah. It's not like he's going to run and tell my feelings to anyone. He's trapped here for the time being, whether either of us like it or not.

Our surroundings have changed with our conversation.

"You did it," I whisper.

Isaiah has brought us down to what appears to be Earth. We stand before the biggest Ferris wheel I've ever seen.

"Come on."

He takes my hand, sending my heart skyrocketing. We walk up metal stairs that creak with every step and take a seat on a red bench contraption. The air smells like fresh rain, though nothing is wet and the skies are as clear as they can be. We buckle ourselves in. Isaiah looks over at me.

"Ready?"

The moment I nod, the ride releases a loud moan that doesn't sound the least bit safe and begins to move. Still, I relax in my seat. We're about a quarter of the way to the top when I speak.

"I'm going to school for a degree I don't want."

Isaiah watches me with a raised brow, but doesn't say anything.

"My sister went to school to become a doctor. She's the..." I hesitate. Am I really about to say that aloud? My deepest, darkest thought? Yes. "She's the pride of the family and can do no wrong." His brows go lax, but his eyes search my face as if he's hunting for my soul. His arm brushes against mine and for a second, I'm too distracted by the heat of it to remember what I was going to say next. "Growing up, any time I voiced my opinion about something, I was always wrong or silly for thinking what I did.

"Soon, I just realized having no opinion was easier. Then I'd never be wrong. Never get in trouble. They'd always be happy."

"But?" Isaiah questions.

"But my parents still aren't happy with me. I'm going to school to follow in their footsteps and somehow it's still not enough." I shrug my shoulders. "I'm making myself miserable for nothing."

That's it. That's all I have to share.

We're at the top of the ride and it slows to a stop. The view around us expands to a nearby city, lit up with twinkling lights in the night sky.

"You gotta buckle up, Chloe. There's only one person livin' your life and that's you. Live it for you and be miserable with your own choices, but don't be miserable 'cause you're following someone else's direction."

Maybe. Maybe he's right.

How did I go so long without Chloe's company? Even though we don't talk about the easiest of topics, I don't think I'd trade this time with her for anything...other than waking up, of course. While I might not have many aspirations, if I did, I wouldn't let someone else get in the way. Well, someone other than myself.

I'm awake early this morning and I'm waiting around for Chloe and Gloria to show up. The room is too quiet without them.

Wait.

Are they here already?

Soft footsteps sound in my room, coming closer and closer. It's only one set. It's almost as if the person is trying to be extremely quiet. A heavy, almost dark, ominous feeling exists to my right. Someone's here and it's not Chloe or Gloria.

I try to quiet down every thought in my brain so I can pay attention to my senses.

Their breathing is soft, but haggard and scratchy.

Almost a wheeze or a rasp. Their exhale is harsh and unhappy. The smell is all wrong. Chloe smells almost like some kind of sweet flower or something. It's soft, subtle, sweet, and calming. Gloria smells like sugar and flour. This...this smells like a person who has been chain smoking two packs a day for fifty years and never tried to wash that pungent, choking smell off their body and clothes.

Who the fuck is in my room?

Just as I feel as if they've gotten even closer to me somehow, I hear the evil nurse save the day.

"Can I help you?" Rita asks in that snarky voice of hers.

The person takes off running.

"Excuse me! Get back here!"

Rita is ignored and she huffs in disdain because of it. "Boy, if I didn't know better, I'd say that was whoever hit you in the first place. Being dressed like that and hightailing it outta here when they were caught."

What?

Could she be right? Is the person back to finish the job? Why now? How'd they find me? As if I'm on the run myself or something. Damn it! Like I need another problem to deal with.

"Oh!"

My attention is dragged back to Rita.

"Can you really hear us? Calm down. It's fine. They are gone. I'll even tell security."

That would make me feel better. Slowly, my heart rate returns to normal.

"Wow. You're one of the most reactive people I've ever seen."

Yeah. If only I'd wake the hell up.

That episode wears me out enough that I am quickly

dragged away to dreamland and off to sleep with an even bigger pit in my stomach.

Some time later, I have a jolting feeling. There's a heavy presence to my left, but nothing to my right. If I could frown, I would. Chloe seems frustrated. Is she on the phone? I can't tell if Gloria is in the room or not.

"Mom, I'm fine. I'm spending all my time with Grandma and we're having a blast. She needs me here. Maybe I should delay school in the fall." There's a long silence. She's definitely on the phone. "No, I'm not saying that, but..." Excitement grabs hold of my heart when I actually feel the warmth of her hand in mine. "I don't know if that's what I want to do."

This time, Chloe is quiet for a long, long time. After a minute or so, she turns her phone to the speaker setting so I can hear both of her parents losing their shit over her one statement of hesitation. I wish I could squeeze her hand. Let her know I'm here for her. That I'm cheering her on. She stood up for herself. Maybe not in a big drastic way. Maybe not in a loud way. But that small step forward is huge for her. The question now is will she continue to do so after this verbal lashing by her parents?

Her parents finally fall silent.

This is it. This is the test.

"Okay. I'll be home in time for school. I'm sorry; I don't know what I was thinking."

The sadness in her voice kills me. Can they not hear it? Do they not care? All I know is I only have a limited amount of time to change Chloe's mind about going home. Not for me. But for her. She should do what she wants with her own life.

But if I'm truly honest, it's for me too.

"Don't look so disappointed," I snap as gently as I can to my grandma. "You heard them." She was standing in the doorway for the last half of my conversation with my parents. "What was I supposed to say?"

"You'll get there, sweet girl. I think you'll make the right decision in the end."

I hope so.

Although I told my parents I'd return home, I'm anxious about doing so. What if Isaiah isn't awake by then? What if he is? What am I supposed to do with this crush I'm developing? Staring at him and his good-looking features doesn't bring me any answers. I want to discuss these things with Grandma, but I'll have to wait until we get home. With Isaiah listening, that's just a bad idea.

"Today is the day," Grandma announces as we leave the hospital.

"For what?" I ask.

"For camping."

Oh. I'm excited and anxious at the same time. It'll be so

odd to be there without Grandpa and with Grandma instead. Then again, he's probably watching over us still. Isaiah has spoken to him, so he's still around in some sense.

Grandma picked a beautiful day for us to do this too. It's warm. There's a nice breeze, but not too much of one that it'll be chilly tonight.

"Sometimes, I wonder what exactly your grandpa needed you to do when he asked you to help that young man," Grandma says softly as we're shopping for some of my camping food favorites. She glances over at me with pinched, concerned eyes. "You're getting very attached to him. You should've seen how reluctant you were to leave him today." Her words are only statements with no negative emotions fueling them.

"I like him," I say. "And I don't understand how I can when we haven't really met. I can't count our meetings so far when it's so bizarre. He may be different when he wakes up. He may not remember me when he wakes up. The connection may not be the same." I tilt my head back and look up at the bland ceiling and say what I'm dreading most of all. "I may not even be here to find out."

Grandma wraps an arm around me and pulls me into her side. "Darling girl, there's a reason your grandpa put the two of you together. We might not know what it is yet, but there's a reason."

"We're running out of time."

"He'll wake up before you leave," she reassures me.

"No, I mean, there's an hourglass and Grandpa said it was important. Something happens when the sand runs out. That's what I meant."

Grandma doesn't know what to say to that, judging by her silence. We continue shopping, grabbing items to make s'mores, and bottles of water, which my Grandpa said was the only sensible drink to have when camping, even though he always snuck in a few bottles of Sun Drop, too.

Today must be a day of doubt. Part of me wonders what in the world I'm even doing. Should I be here with Grandma or should I be with Isaiah?

"Should I even keep seeing him?" I ask my next thought aloud.

Grandma looks at me as if I'm crazy for even asking. "You're supposed to be doing this, Chloe. I can feel it in my bones. Isaiah is going to change your life and you his. Grandpa had a reason for all of this; don't forget that."

I wish I knew what that reason was.

When we get back to Grandma's, she sets us right to work on getting the tent put up. She sends me up to the dusty attic for the air mattress. The heat is stifling up there. I'm only up there for a few seconds before I feel as if I can't breathe. Small beads of sweat build on my forehead. I quickly hobble over to the corner where I last put the air mattress. The attic isn't tall enough for me to stand upright fully. As soon as the box is in my hands, I run back.

The cool air hits me fast. Ah. Freedom. I drop the box and let it hit the floor before crawling down. I wish Isaiah was here. My grandpa too. I bet they would enjoy helping us set everything up and then later, they'd enjoy hanging out together. This tradition that I had with Grandpa can continue, but it won't be the same. But at least I'll still have it. Peace fills my soul as I take a deep breath. My eyes roam over the backyard and our completed setup.

Grandma is right; things will all work out in the end.

WHEN I APPEAR in dreamland tonight, it's as if I'm falling into it. I scream as I free fall. The sound echos and pierces my own eardrums. As if it's amplified. The wind blasting past me burns my skin. Hair slaps my face. The ground appears closer and closer. Why couldn't I just appear as I normally do? I squeeze my eyes closed as I spot Isaiah. He's going to watch me die unless something changes before I hit the ground. A horrifying thought hits me: Will I die in real life too?

"Chloe!" Isaiah yells.

Air sucks out of my lungs as I fall with a thud.

On top of Isaiah who tried to catch me. But the force of my incoming landing has knocked him down as well.

"Are you okay?" he asks, using a hand on either side of my face to push my hair back. I nod, my throat feeling hoarse. "What the hell was that?" I shake my head. "Are you sure you're okay?"

Before I can answer, a loud crack draws our attention to the hourglass. We watch in horror as the glass along the crack in the upper globe separates just enough that sand now falls from there as well. We're losing more time.

I bury my face in the crook of Isaiah's neck. I don't understand what's happening. Why are we being placed under this kind of pressure without even knowing what we're supposed to be accomplishing?

He runs his hands up and down my back. "It's okay. We'll figure it out."

I lift my head to look at him. The realization that I'm still lying on top of him hits me hard. A full body blush seems to start from my toes and run up to my cheeks. Isaiah smiles a little smirk at me.

"Yes, Chloe?"

"I should probably get up."

"I kind of like you where you are."

My eyes widen at his suddenly husky voice and forwardness.

"Too much?" he asks upon seeing my expression.

I shake my head no, even though I'm not sure. With my answer, however, Isaiah places the bed beneath us instead of the cloud-like ground. My hands are placed on either side of his head from where I was trying to brace my fall. I drop to my elbows, which brings my face even closer to his.

"How was your day?" he asks.

"Good. Grandma and I went shopping and then camped out in the backyard."

"That's nice."

We fall silent with only the noise of the sand falling to disturb what little peace we should have. Isaiah lifts his head an inch, his eyes roam my face, and then he lifts it another inch. And another. His lips are a breath away from mine. Will he really kiss me?

Three long, solid seconds go by where neither of us say a word.

This is too much. I don't know if I can do this. I don't know if I want to kiss him here.

"How was your day?" I dumbly ask while awkwardly rolling off of him.

Isaiah laughs. "Well, I went runnin', swimmin', even took a day trip to the beach."

I eye him, trying not to laugh, but can't help myself. "Very funny."

"You asked," he points out. But then his brows pinch together.

"What is it?" I ask as I prop myself up on my elbow to look at him.

"Someone came to visit me today and then ran off when the nurse came in."

My eyes widen. "What?"

Isaiah nods as he stares up at the night sky. "It was not a good feeling while they were there. The nurse has told security at least. Not much else I can do." He sighs. "I need to wake up." He rolls onto his side and sets those troubled hazel eyes on me.

"Don't you wonder what will happen once you wake up?"

He shrugs one shoulder. "You mean when we're fully real and not part of our imaginations or whatever the hell this is? You think we'll be different?"

"I'm just worried is all."

Isaiah nods. "It's been a bit of a day for you. Why don't you get some rest?"

I can't argue with that and sleep sounds nice.

9

I'm worried I won't wake up. Something feels off lately. I don't know how to describe it other than I feel different. Maybe the hourglass is counting down to when something will happen within my body and I'll officially die. Or maybe something will happen and I'll be destined to spend my life like this.

That can't happen.

I have to wake up so I can see my brother. So I can take care of him. I have to wake up. But why am I feeling different? Could it be a sign that I'll wake up? Wouldn't I be feeling more positive and good in general? Because I don't. I almost told Chloe about it last night, but after everything that happened, I couldn't bring myself to do it. Things are changing and we don't have answers. I don't want to worry her even more.

Being like this is really pissing me off, though. Things were a bit of a blur day in and day out before Chloe. Now, though, I feel more conscious. If I'm not thinking about Chloe, my mind is on my brother. It's eating me alive that he is likely thinking the worst of me right now. While I could send word via Chloe, it's out of the question.

Unless...

But should I? It's not really her place. It would give me some peace of mind, though. Who knows how long I'll be here. Do I really want my brother to go even longer without knowing what's going on with me?

"Why are you pacing?"

I whirl around and see Chloe. "Hey, you didn't fall from the sky today."

"Are you okay?" she asks, ignoring my statement.

"Maybe." I step toward her, but she takes a step back.

"What's going on?" She glances over at the hourglass, but it hasn't sustained any more damage since we were here last.

"If I asked a favor of you, would you do it exactly as I asked?"

There's a heartbeat of silence between us before she nods. "What is it?"

"I want you to tell my brother, but I need you to do it only as I say and how I say."

Her shoulders release tension I didn't realize she was carrying for me. "Of course. Tell me what to do." She steps closer to me. My gift for answering her question. I ignore that and focus on my mission.

"It would be easier if he was in school, but he's not right now. Our best shot is catching him when he meets up with his best friend." It's his only friend, but I don't mention that. "If you see him getting dropped off, do not approach him until after his foster parents leave. His name is Jeremiah. His best friend is Mark. Tell him what happened to me and where I am. If he doesn't believe you, tell him I told you about the time he tried to make a squirrel his pet. He named him Earl. Earl the Squirrel. Just make sure he knows I didn't abandon him." Ever since Chloe first mentioned how she could do this for me, that's been nagging at me. That he'd be devastated at the thought I'd completely given up on him and abandoned him. I can't let him think that a second longer. I hurry on to tell her where Mark lives, feeling like I'm running out of time. "Will you do it?" I ask.

Chloe opens her mouth to respond, but the ground beneath us shakes and rumbles. Fear brightens her eyes. Before I can reach for her hand, she's yanked by an invisible force backward and up into the air.

The moment she disappears, the ground stops. Another crack opens up in the hourglass as a pain so startling and severe hits me in the chest. Then, I'm pulled out of our place as well.

10

CHLOE

I awaken with a start. What the hell just happened? Is Isaiah okay? I feel like he isn't. Some ingrained sense deep down tells me he's in trouble. My hand can't stop rubbing my sternum either. The pain is nearly unbearable, but it doesn't overwhelm my desire to see Isaiah and make sure he's okay. Without thinking too much about it, I get out of bed and dress. I debate whether or not I should wake my grandma. She's been through enough as it is. Waking her up in the middle of the night in a panic over Isaiah won't do her any good. Instead, I make sure to leave a note, find her keys, and hightail it out of here.

Nothing makes sense, which isn't surprising. I don't like how our visits in dreamland are changing, though. It makes me nervous. I can't seem to stop rubbing my chest as if that might ease the pain and anxiety.

The activity inside of Isaiah's room doesn't help the chest pains.

I try to make my way in, but a nurse spots me and immediately ushers me out.

"What happened? What's wrong?"

"Please wait here," she orders before closing the door of his room in my face with a hard and loud thud in the otherwise quiet hospital floor.

The noises inside sound like something terrible has happened.

God, my chest hurts. I lean against the wall, waiting to be let inside. The pain pulses like a live wire. It causes me to double over. It's wave over wave of pain that drags me to the floor, tears spilling from my eyes, until it suddenly stops. I gasp for breath, unsure if I should feel relieved or not.

All I can do then is breathe heavily while the residue of the memory of pain lingers in my chest. It curls around my ribs. The threat of it returning is present with every breath. Ten minutes after my pain ends, nurses and doctors begin to file out of Isaiah's room. I manage to stand up and grab one nurse by the arm.

"What happened?"

This nurse is one of the nicer ones. Her eyes are tired and a little sad. "We just lost him—"

I rush into the room, my heart already shattered and tears falling freely. No. It can't be. I'd know it.

The monitor beeps as per usual and his chest rises and falls. Never thought I'd love that sound. Or that it'd bring such relief. He's okay. He's here. He's alive. Oh, thank God. I nearly crumble onto the bed next to him.

"For two minutes," the nurse finishes from a few steps behind me. "They'll be running tests on him soon to try and figure out why he coded. I checked on him ten minutes prior and he was stable. It doesn't make any sense to me."

"Can I stay with him?"

"Until they're ready to do the tests, absolutely."

She leaves without any further words to me.

All I can do at first is watch Isaiah. Make sure the heart

monitor beeps with his heartbeat. Watch his chest to make sure it continues to rise and fall with his breathing. He's okay. A moment of hesitation and I find myself crawling into his bed with him, being careful not to really disturb him.

"I don't want to fall asleep ever again if this is what happens," I whisper to him.

His heartbeat accelerates.

"You died," I tell him, my tears falling once more. Just saying those words makes me feel hollow. "Maybe we should wait for you to talk to me when you wake up. It's not ideal, I know that, but this is starting to get scary, Isaiah. There are too many unknowns." I take a deep breath. "No decisions until I see you again," I promise, which slowly causes his heartbeat to return to normal. "I wish you'd wake up already," I whisper.

We lie in relative silence for a bit before a nurse comes in and tells me it's time for me to go. Leaving him after the ordeal we've had tonight is the hardest thing I've had to do. I walk to the double automatic sliding doors, but stop. I don't want to leave him. Honestly, I'm not sure my feet will take me one more step in any direction away from him. I should go home, though. Right? But what if it's a bad idea? There's a sinking feeling in my stomach that causes me to turn around and return to his room to wait. I curl up in my chair with a blanket, hoping everything turns out to be okay.

"Chloe, dear." Between the words and having my shoulder lightly shaken, I wake up to see my grandma leaning over me.

That is startling enough, considering I left her at home. "Grandma? What are you doing here? How'd you get here?"

I push myself up in the chair, see Isaiah made it back to his room, and then I see my worst nightmare.

My sister.

"What are you doing here?"

"You freaked her out and I had to drive all the way to Lupine Grove to bring her here." She waves her arms around in confusion. "What the hell is going on?"

My eyes flash back to my grandma's. "Didn't you get my note? I left it on the fridge."

Grandma's eyes crinkle. "No, Chloe. I didn't see anything. What happened? Is Isaiah okay?"

"Is anyone going to tell me what the hell we're doing here?" Marie demands. "Who is Isaiah?"

Of all the people my grandma could've called for help, she had to call little miss perfect Marie? Now we have to explain things to her.

"Isaiah is a friend of ours," I say as I nod my head toward where he lies on the bed.

Marie frowns. "How do you have a friend here? How long has he been like this?"

Before I can stop her, my grandma launches into the whole sordid tale. When Marie finds out my parents don't know, I can see the evil glint in her eyes. Or maybe I'm imagining it. Either way, she thinks we've both lost our minds.

But what has started to loop in my mind is that I went to sleep.

And didn't meet Isaiah while I was there.

What. The. Hell?

I f Chloe slept here, then why didn't we meet in our place? What is going on?

"Grandma is fine now; can you please leave?" I hear Chloe ask the new person in the room.

"I drove an hour to pick her up, bring her here, and then I find out you've coerced Grandma into something crazy! I'm calling Mom."

"Marie!" Chloe whisper-shouts.

"Let her go. Tell me what happened," Gloria insists.

Things are quiet for a moment and then I listen to Chloe's voice return to that scared, unsure tone it was last night as she recounts what happened, even that I died.

"I'm sorry, Grandma. I just couldn't bear to leave him alone. I'm going to have my hands full with Mom and Dad soon. Will you stay here with him? I need to find his brother while I can force myself to leave him."

She's going to find my brother? Part of me is relieved but with the recent turn of events, I'd be lying if I said I wasn't nervous too. Maybe it's better that he thinks I disappeared or died in an alley somewhere. That way, if I'm wrong and I do die, he won't have to go through that heartache all over again.

All of a sudden things go black.

A SECOND LATER, I'm in our place.

And so is Chloe's grandfather.

"What's happening?" I ask. "I died."

Daniel wears a solemn look. "I know, Isaiah. I come with a message."

"From who? You or someone else?" Without meaning to, my eyes glance toward the sky.

Daniel shrugs. "You have one week before your fate is decided."

"My fate?" My eyes widen. "You mean I might not wake up?" How is that even a possibility? I've been so sure all this time that there was only one outcome and now I might not wake up?

"You must tell Chloe about the deadline."

"Why should I worry her?" I ask.

"I can't say, but that is how it has to be. If you don't tell her, there will be consequences." He looks concerned and that looks bad enough.

"So I'll see her again?"

"Of course."

That makes me relax.

A boom of thunder causes me to whirl around to face the hourglass. The crack lengthens toward the base of the upper bulb. More sand falls to the ground, disappearing into low-lying clouds.

Time is running out.

12

CHLOE

W hat in the world am I doing? This is ten thousand miles out of my comfort zone. I want to turn around and run back to the comfort of Isaiah's hospital room.

But I can't. Isaiah needs me to do this. Thank goodness Jeremiah's friend lives in town, otherwise this would be impossible. I parked a little ways down the road in front of the town library and am sitting on a bench. My eyes are peeled for any sign for a boy looking like Isaiah going to the house I keep glancing toward.

A bundle of bouncing nerves sinks to the deepest pit of my stomach when a car pulls up in front of the house. With a deep breath, I watch to see if anyone will get out. Yep. There he is. This is it. The car speeds off the moment Jeremiah closes the door. Still, I wait until it feels safe enough to stand and jog toward him.

"Excuse me!" I shout when I'm close enough. He sort of looks like Isaiah. He's at the right house. It's either his brother or the friend. The young boy turns around with a scowl prominent on his face. "Jeremiah?" I tentatively ask as I finish approaching him.

His scowl hardens. "Who are you?"

"I'm here with news about your brother, Isaiah." I thought the entire way over about what might be the best opening and figured that was both appealing and vague enough to hook him.

Jeremiah glances at his friend's house, both ways up the street, and then back to me. "How do you know my brother?" There's a faint glint of hope in his eyes, but he's trying so hard not to let it show in his voice.

"I'm a friend of his. My name is Chloe. I have a bit of a weird relationship with him."

His eyes harden. "What do you want? Isaiah dropped off the face of the earth and forgot all about me. Why are you here instead of him? How do I even know you really know him and this isn't some weird setup?"

"He told me about Earl the Squirrel," I blurt out.

Jeremiah stares at me for a long moment and after a solid minute his shoulders relax and release their tension. "Where is he?"

"He hasn't abandoned you; he was hit by a car and has been in a coma. He's been in the hospital for almost two months."

If it's possible, he seems to relax even further somehow while also seizing with fear. His eyes widen. "Is he going to be okay?"

I nod. "Absolutely." I don't know for sure, but some way, he will be. He has to be.

Jeremiah rocks back and forth on his heels. He curses under his breath as he glances at his friend's front door again. "I don't know if I can come see him."

"That's okay. They say he can hear us when we talk to

him; I'll tell him I was able to find you and that you wish you could come see him. I'm sure he's been worried about you. Have you been okay?"

He shrugs.

Before I left the hospital, I found a piece of paper and wrote my cell number on it. I pull it out of my pocket now and hold it out to Jeremiah. "If you need anything at all at any time of day, call me. I know you don't know me, but Isaiah was working so hard to get to where he could get you back. He might not be able to really be here for you now, but I can. Please don't hesitate to call if you need anything."

"Thanks. I need to go." He quickly turns and jogs to his friend's door before disappearing inside without even knocking.

There.

Met his brother. Gave him the news. Tried to let him know he could rely on me. Isaiah should be proud. I hope everything will be okay now. Or that he can at least relax.

Just as I'm parked in the hospital parking lot, I get a call from my parents. Marie probably called them the moment she knew they'd be awake and they decided to call me as soon as they hung up with her.

"What is going on over there, Chloe?" Mom launches as soon as a hello leaves my mouth. "You're supposed to be keeping an eye on your grandmother while she grieves. But you're dragging her back to the very place she lost her husband for some comatose person no one knows? Is this why you're trying to wiggle your way out of school?"

"Mom," I start.

"No, Marie explained it to us. It's clear that you've lost your mind! Bless your heart, you never know what you want and the few times you do, it's always the wrong decision."

"Mom!" If my ears could bleed from her words, blood

would be pouring down my neck, falling and falling until it pools at my feet. I want it to stop. Why can't they ever leave me alone? But she won't stop talking.

"We want you to come home. You're better off here. Obviously, you're not doing your grandmother much good." On and on she goes.

What would Isaiah do?

He's probably tell her exactly what he's thinking, but I can't do that. I glance around at all the cars. Some folks getting in or out. I want to be inside.

I could hang up.

My heart skips a beat just at the thought of it. The imaginary pool of blood grows and grows. Soon, it'll start filling up the car until it drowns me. As if I'm on autopilot, I pull the phone away from my ear and stare at it. Mom is still ranting. My thumb moves over and hovers over the red icon. With a deep breath and before I can chicken out, I quickly push the button.

Oh god.

What have I done?

I turn my phone off before they can call back and the pressure of answering hits me. I did two things today that were totally not me and that's enough for a lifetime, it feels like. With that done, I hurry inside.

"How is he doing?" I ask when I burst into his room.

Grandma gives me a brief look before returning her gaze to her crochet. "He's fine. How are you?"

"I just hung up on Mom, so I'm frazzled."

Her eyebrows pop up, but she smiles. "Good for you. I'm sure Isaiah agrees."

I groan at how happy and at ease she is over this. "I'm going to be in such trouble."

Grandma rolls her eyes. "Sugar, you're twenty-two. You

never got in trouble in your teens. This is definitely the time to get in trouble; it's the last decade until you're my age," she says with a wink. When her humor bounces right off me, she releases a little sigh, rests her crochet work on the edge of Isaiah's bed, and leans toward me. "Chloe, sweet girl, I'm only going to remind you of this one more time. You have to live your life for yourself and your wants and needs, no matter how scary that is for you. Stand up for yourself and find your voice *now*," she stresses heavily, her gaze clear and piercing. "If you don't do it now, it'll only get harder."

Talking the talk is easy, but walking the walk is what I'm going to struggle with. I don't know what to say because I don't want to make any promises. Instead, I get comfy in my seat.

"Whoa. You must be tired to fall asleep while you're with me. Once I realized you were snoozin', I tried to doze off myself to see if I could make it here too." Isaiah looks around as if to make sure everything is in its place. "Glad everything looks normal."

My eyes roam over his body. "I don't even know where to start."

Isaiah smiles and pulls me into a hug. "I do. I'm thrilled to hear about you hangin' up on your mom. I hope she gasped and her jaw hit the damn floor."

I laugh. "I'm sure she was very dramatic about it. It didn't feel good to me though."

"You'll get there, Chloe." He squeezes me one last time before releasing me. His eyes rest briefly on my lips and then lift to meet my gaze. Isaiah clears his throat. He rocks on his heels and stuffs his hands into his pockets. "How's my brother? Did you find him?"

"Yes," I say with a nod. "He's okay. He said he didn't know if he would be able to see you, but I told him that would be okay. That I'd tell you he wished he could come. He seemed relieved to hear that you're alive." This next part, I'm not too sure if he's okay with, but I don't want to lie. "I gave him my number. I told him since you aren't available at the moment that if he ever needs anything, he could, uh, call me." I hold my breath, trying to read his expression, but getting nothing. "Is that okay?"

Isaiah pulls me into another hug, but this time it's bone crushing. "Thank you. Not that I want you involved in any way, but…" He honestly seems at a loss for words. "Thanks, Chloe."

"Welcome," I whisper, totally overwhelmed by his gratitude.

He lets me go and frowns as the ground rumbles. "Right," he mutters. "I had another visit from your grandfather. He said I have a week until my fate is decided."

I stumble backward a step. *A week?*

"Yes, a week."

I said that aloud? My heart races as the mere thought of what all this might mean. "Why did he say fate? Why couldn't he just say you'd wake up next week?"

Isaiah folds his arms over his chest with a frown on his face. "I don't like it either. But he said I had to tell you."

I grab the front of his shirt, feeling slightly panicky. "Isaiah, you have to wake up. I told Jeremiah that you'd be fine. Don't make me a liar."

He takes hold of my wrists. His thumb rubs over my skin in a light gentle manner that's surprisingly calming. "I'll wake up." His words are firm and strong. They are so sure that I actually believe him.

"Okay." Slowly, I uncurl my fingers and Isaiah lets go of his hold as well. Our arms drop to our sides. "Are we going to talk about you almost dying completely?"

He actually almost chuckles and shakes his head. "Nope.

I'm alive and kickin' and that's all there is to it. Let's not tempt fate by remindin' her that she didn't get me the second time around." He tilts his head with a faint smile. "Probably more than the second, really."

I shake my head at how blasé he is about dying and all these near-death experiences.

"I feel like we should get out of here," he says as his gaze strays to the ever-present hourglass. "Where do you want to go?"

I shrug my shoulders. "Surprise me."

Isaiah grins. "Close your eyes. I'm going big today."

Wordlessly and without hesitation, I close my eyes. He takes my hands again and I wait. And wait. After a moment, Isaiah curses, but then, it happens. Heat, sunshine maybe, is warm and cozy against my skin. The heady fragrance of sunscreen, salt, and pure beach fills my lungs. Almost too hot sand cradles my feet. My toes automatically wiggle deeper. Birds caw and waves crash and fizzle. A cool breeze ruffles my hair across my shoulders. Bare shoulders.

My eyes pop open. I look down at myself. I'm in a bikini! A stupid yellow polka dotted bikini, too! I gawk at myself and then Isaiah.

"Didn't know that'd happen," he mutters, his eyes eating up every inch of skin now on display.

But he's in swim trunks too. I'm first distracted by the lightly defined muscles. Then I notice the scars; how did I not notice them before? They seem to be everywhere. Are they all from the accident?

"Ask."

My gaze flings up to Isaiah's. His smile is gone, but he doesn't seem upset.

"Not all from the accident?"

He shakes his head. "Some are from foster parents." He

points to a random one on his forearm. "Some are from dumb shit I did while high." He points to one that drags across his ribcage. "Do they bother you?"

"No," I quickly answer. "I'm more bothered by this." I motion to myself, which makes Isaiah laugh.

"Trust me, you have nothin' to be bothered about." He gives me one last look over before nodding toward the ocean. "Let's swim." Without waiting to see if I'll follow, he jogs toward the water.

After one more look at myself, wishing I was in something I'd be more comfortable wearing, I take off after him. He takes us out where the water is a bit calmer, but not too far away from shore to be nervous. We float facing once another and nerves begin to bubble in my stomach.

"Tell me a secret," Isaiah says after a moment.

"Are you going to tell me one?"

He nods. "Sure."

I think for a moment, trying to decide what to share.

"Something no one else knows," he adds.

I frown at this added complication. It's not like I have much of a life to start with. Not one of my own. How many secrets can a girl like that have? Very few, if any. Apparently, I'm taking too long. Isaiah grabs ahold of my hips. It startles me at first, but his hands are sure and steady, the most reassuring thing I feel right now. He looks like he'd wait a hundred years if that's how long it takes for me to open my mouth and spill my guts.

It only takes two minutes, though.

"When I was ten, my sister made this announcement at dinner once night that she was going to be a doctor. She was sixteen then. And my parents were so thrilled that she was so firm in what she wanted to pursue in life. But I remember sitting there and crumbling on the inside. My parents had always been hard on me, but that was the night I knew it was always going to be bad. Mom looked at me and her eyes got sad like she knew I'd never make it in the medical field, even if I'd wanted to do that.

"She patted my hand and said, 'Don't worry, Chloe. We'll find something suitable for you to do. You don't have to be like Marie.' Marie got to make the decision on her own, but me? My parents knew when I was ten that they were going to have to pick my life's choices for me. Sometimes, I feel like I'm still this ten-year-old girl who never grew up, and honestly, I worry that when I'm forty, I'm going to be this pathetic woman who still lives with her parents because they don't trust her to live on her own and I can't get out from under them."

There. That's off my chest. My ever growing fear that I'm going to be the weird woman version of a forty-year-old virgin who lives in her parents' basement is out in the world. Or at least this one.

Isaiah squeezes my hips. "That's not going to happen," he replies in a low, firm voice. "One day, you'll cuss your parents out and go to school for what *you* want to do," he reassures, smiling when he thinks of me cussing them out.

"Your turn." That's all I can manage to say. Not to mention, I'm a bit ready to move on from this bit of conversation.

Isaiah lets go of my hips and backs away from me a bit. He tilts his head back as if he needs strength from the sun. But then his eyes meet mine. They always do. "Only one other person knows this, actually. I, uh..." He exhales heavily. The disappointment rolls off of him as strong as the waves currently crashing to shore. "I relapsed the night of the accident. Things were getting fucking difficult when it came to my brother and the pressure was building." Isaiah winces. "I was two days away from finding out if they were going to let Jeremiah live with me or not. I got into an argument with my best friend over it and went wandering the streets to walk it off." He shrugs his shoulders as if the rest is history.

So he has lied to me.

He was high when he was hit.

"It's been eating me alive. I probably wouldn't be here if I hadn't gave in to the craving."

"Wait. Shouldn't your friend have looked for you in the hospitals then?" I ask.

"She wouldn't look in case she'd find me dead."

"She?" I blurt. His best friend is a girl? This weird feeling grasps my heart and I don't like it one bit. I don't feel comfortable with this idea, that he's really a she, and I don't like what that might say about me, but there it is.

Isaiah grins. "Jealous?"

I narrow my eyes and shove him away. "That would require me liking you, and I don't."

He laughs. *Laughs.* A true, he's tickled pink, laugh. It's beautiful. "Yeah, okay, Chloe. Whatever you say."

"You're pushing your luck, Isaiah," I warn. Am I flirting? It almost feels like it.

"Been doin' that my whole life. But on a serious note—"

Before he can finish, the ocean suddenly becomes turbulent. The sky darkens with big black clouds. Huge waves surge up right on top of us and crash on our heads.

"Don't...let...go!" Isaiah gasps through each wave, holding my hand so tight, my knuckles rub together painfully.

Water burns a path up my nose as I'm pulled back under, gulping a mouth full of salt water. Just as I break the surface, the water begins circling like a massive whirlpool. The water moves faster and faster. If possible, I feel like it's pulling us apart. There's a loud crack of thunder. The water sucks me under, yanking me away from Isaiah. I hear Isaiah scream my name, full of terror.

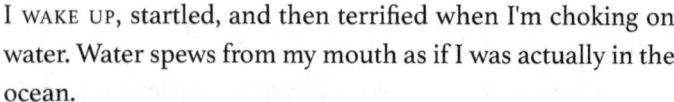

I WAKE UP, startled, and then terrified when I'm choking on water. Water spews from my mouth as if I was actually in the ocean.

"Chloe?"

Grandma rushes over as the last of the water seems to leave my mouth. "What in the world?" she asks, patting my back as I cough.

But then Isaiah begins to cough and convulse. Grandma abandons me in a heartbeat, not that I mind, to call a nurse into the room. Water gushes out of his mouth, around his ventilator. His heart rate soars sky high. A crowd of people rush into the room. Their confusion is clear, but they get to work. I watch in horror as they remove his ventilator. What if he stops breathing completely? Not that he's having any luck right now.

One last spew of water coats his chin and chest. His body relaxes. Everyone holds their breath and watches. Will he keep breathing? Will he die? What will happen?

His heartbeat returns to normal. And his chest still rises and falls.

Holy moly. He's breathing on his own!

"Do y'all mind..." a nurse trails off when she sees my equally wet shirt.

"She spilled a drink on herself," Grandma explains. "We'll give y'all a few minutes. C'mon, Chloe."

Reluctantly, I leave the room.

My grandma grabs my wrist and pulls me to a quiet nook. "What in God's green Earth happened?"

"We're running out of time. The place we go to is starting to be dangerous." That much is clear. "We were trying to have a fun little escape, but that didn't go so well." I glance down the hall. "But maybe it is. He's breathing on his own." For now at least. So much has happened just in the last day. Some good. Some not. The not hits me hard. "Is Marie still here?"

"She's at my house right now."

I hand Grandma her keys back. "Try and get rid of her then. I'm going to stay here with Isaiah."

The pursed lips and hand on her hip give me a pretty good indication that she wants me to come with her. The question is do I want to argue with her? I'm wiped as it is. It's unwise to argue with my grandma unless you really want to fight for whatever it is. She's relentless, so you have to be even more so than she.

She stares me down until my shoulders give.

"Fine," I groan. "But I'm not dealing with Marie." Because inside I'm a four-year-old who refuses to play nice with her sister.

We wait a few minutes to see if we can check on Isaiah, but a nurse lets us know that it's going to be a while. Grandma leads me out. It feels as if there is an invisible hand yanking on my ear all the way out. No matter what happens next, it won't be good.

13

S omething is different. I've been in and out of my own version of consciousness for what feels like forever. My last solid memory was hearing a bunch of talking, machines in distress, and this horrible feeling that I was drowning in real life just as I was in our place. And now?

I can't tell exactly what it is, but something feels different. Better.

But my room is quiet. Quieter than before. I don't know if that's a good thing or a bad thing. For the moment, I'm going with bad because Chloe isn't here. She probably had to head home.

I hate that I released one of my secrets, but at the same time it feels good to get it off my chest. Then everything went to hell. Chloe might have the right idea about trying to avoid our place, but I'm not sure how we do that. I'm pulled there every time I go to sleep. Even before I met Chloe, I was there. As long as I've been in this hospital, that's where I've gone.

Something shifts in my room. A presence that comes with footsteps. They stop on the side of my bed.

The person is quiet for a long time. And then a throat clears. "Hey, Isaiah."

If I could sigh with relief, I would. My brother is here. I'm partially worried because he shouldn't be here, but there's not much I can do about it either.

"Uh, that girl, Chloe? She told me that you might could hear me. I can't stay long, but I had to come see for myself." He's quiet for a moment and then he says, "I'm glad you're okay." His voice cracks. "Things are worse. I need you to wake up and come get me, Isaiah. Or else I'm running away."

There's a slight buzzing noise, but it only lasts a few seconds. Jeremiah curses, says a quick goodbye, and footsteps hurry out of my room. As if the urgency to wake up wasn't placing a massive amount of pressure on me already, the pressure just became bone crunching.

If I could will myself awake, I'd be awake already. It's as if Chloe and I are supposed to accomplish something, but what? I've given her some of my trust. We've shared some dark things about ourselves. We've gotten closer. What more does it want from us? What more are we supposed to do? Have we not given enough already? It took years for me to get to this place with my best friend. I managed to put most of my skepticism aside so I could wake the fuck up. Yet here I am!

Why?

Maybe this is punishment for what happened the night of the accident that landed me in here in the first place. Either way, I hope Daniel appears the next time I go to our place. I will demand answers. I need to wake up and get back to my brother.

14

CHLOE

"You both need to be thrown into a psych ward!" Marie shouts as she paces in front of us. Grandma and I sit on her couch, calm as ever.

Well, Grandma is calm. I'm about to burst.

"There is no need to yell," Grandma replies sternly. "All I asked for was a ride, not your opinion." That stops Marie in her tracks, her feet swiveling slowly on her heels as she turns to look at Grandma. Her mouth hangs agape. "Marie, you're a sweet girl, but we have this handled. This is something you can't understand. We don't need a babysitter and I'm sure you have better things to do." Grandma stands and wipes her hands as if literally wiping her hands of the conversation. "Now, I'll fix dinner and you're more than welcome to eat with us before you head home." Grandma moves toward the kitchen, her slippers sliding against the floor as she walks. She doesn't lift her legs all that well sometimes.

The room is silent for all of two seconds.

"Why do you do this to our family, Chloe?" My sister sounds both utterly exhausted and curious.

"Do what?" I ask, slightly confused, but mostly scared. I'm not sure I can take another verbal beating so soon after the last one from my parents.

"Why can't you just be a good daughter? Stop worrying everyone and do what is asked of you. Stay in the lines, Chloe."

That's what I've done my entire life and it's still not good enough. Why should I keep trying? If the disappointment will be there either way, maybe I should just run full speed ahead in the direction I want. Well, maybe not full speed because I'm not that brave, but a decent jogging pace will do. If I don't do something now, I never will.

"Shut up." My firm, even-keeled voice interrupts Marie's continuing rant.

She stops short and stares at me much like she did Grandma.

Each word must be forced, but I power through. "What I decide to do with my life is no one's business. Stay out of it." That's it. Seems small, but it's a giant leap for me. A rush of pride and relief floods through me. Now if I can only tell my parents the same thing.

"Fine." Marie throws her hands up in the air. "Whatever happens is on you. I'm going home." She tells Grandma bye and walks out.

I wish I could tell Isaiah what I've done. About my newest accomplishment. He might just be a bigger cheer-leader for me than Grandma, if only because he's more vocal. Time is ticking down for us. My biggest fear is the unknown of whether he'll remember us when he wakes up. What then?

"Chloe, sweet girl?" Grandma calls.

I hurry to the kitchen, hoping she has something for me to do. She stands at the stove, stirring something in a pot.

"I can hear you worrying all the way in here. Get your crochet, keep working on that blanket, and try to relax."

Well, that's disappointing. "You don't need help?"

She laughs. "Not with that kind of anxiety in the room. Go on now." She makes a shooing motion with her hand before completely ignoring my presence.

I groan, but do as she says. Maybe it'll help. If I'm really going to do this, then I need to do some thinking anyway. As I sit in the recliner with my crochet project in my lap, slowly working through it, I think. Probably too hard. If I do this, go against my parents, that includes going for what I want in life. Becoming a teacher simply isn't one of those things.

But what is?

One reason it was so easy to go along with what they wanted is because I haven't the slightest idea of what I want to do with my life. But I know what I don't want to do. When you've never really been allowed to have passions in life, how does one choose what do to with their life? That is the pressing question.

SLEEP WAS RESTLESS. Isaiah and I didn't meet. I don't know what that means, but I don't like it. I try to convince Grandma to stay behind, simply drop me off, but she refuses. She's as invested in this as I am. The nurse we initially didn't like is there.

She actually smiles at us today. I watch as she performs her duties with care, giving us her report as she does so. By the end, though, Rita's smile fades.

"He keeps getting a visitor, though. The person was here again this morning. Way early. I think it's a woman, but I can't be sure. Anyway, she was in here when I started my shift and did my first set of rounds. When I found her in here and spoke to her, she ran out and pushed me into the wall, trying to get around me." She pauses and wrings her hands. "I keep informing security because the behavior is weird at best, but I thought y'all might want to know as well."

The person was back. This is not good. Isaiah thought that person was dangerous. As if we need something else to worry about! I take my seat next to Isaiah's bed while Grandma thanks Rita and she heads out to continue her work.

"I don't mean to pile on the bad news, but..." Grandma and I look at one another. "Your parents are flying in today." I groan. "You've freaked them out, sweet girl. It's now or never. Time to fight or time to roll over like a dog." She shrugs as she takes her seat and pulls out her crochet project.

"You don't sound so confident in me, Grandma."

"It's not that," she insists. "You just don't do well with direct confrontation, dear."

And there is a lot of direct confrontation coming my way. My stomach has been in knots since the mere mention of my parents. I need to come up with a plan and I need to do it before they arrive. I look over at Isaiah. I wish I could talk to him about this. Maybe he'd have some helpful advice.

There are a few things I already know for sure about my future, which my parents aren't going to like.

I don't want to continue on the educational path I'm on currently.

I think that maybe, possibly, it might be a good idea to maybe move out of my parents' house. I guess. Maybe. I'm not sure. The idea sounds appealing, but the ripple effects where my parents are concerned seem like they will be disastrous. I'm not above working to make this happen. The issue comes primarily with the question of whether I'm brave enough for this. That is still under review.

Then there is the problem of my career path. What am I going to do there?

"Chloe, I think his pillows have been fluffed enough for the last ten minutes. Not to mention, the nurse already fluffed them."

I frown as I place them just so back underneath his head.

"Something on your mind?" Grandma asks.

"What isn't?" I mutter, causing her to raise an eyebrow at me. "A career," I add.

She only nods and continue to work on her blanket. Nervous and worried, I continue to fiddle with Isaiah's sheets, his hands, and trying to distract myself by wondering if he's comfortable. At least, he looks better. Not quite as pale.

"Maybe you should be a nurse. You fuss over him and watch the nurses like a hawk enough that you should be able to do their jobs," she finishes with a chuckle.

A nurse? Just because I like to care for Isaiah doesn't mean I'd want to be a nurse. Right? I'm not sure. But it won't hurt to add it to my short list of possibilities. I curl up in my chair to give Isaiah some space. My nerves are antsy still, so I decide to do a search on my phone to see if the internet will be any help in deciding my fate. There are a lot of tests. Some of them seem dumb as dirt as my Grandma would say, but I surprisingly get some good ideas to add to my list to look into further. The only thing appealing about being a teacher was the idea of helping others. All of the jobs on my list have that trait as well.

I feel oddly accomplished, although I haven't actually done anything.

That feelings bursts when Grandma and I arrive back to her place to find my angry parents, who pull in behind us in a rental car.

"Go take a little nap while I start dinner. That'll give you some peace for a while longer," Grandma says as we both spot the frowns on their faces. That sounds great to me. I hurry inside.

Sleep also sounds great because maybe I'll be able to meet with Isaiah. But I go to my room, lie on my bed, and stare at my ceiling for almost an hour and a half before my grandma comes to retrieve me.

"How do they seem?" I ask when she tells me it's time.

"You just remember to fight for what you want."

Okay. That means it's bad. I nod in response to her. "I think we should lie about Isaiah."

"You do what you think is best, dear, and I'll back you up. Now, come on."

She turns and leaves me to follow. Reluctantly, I will Isaiah to lend me some strength. I will surely need it.

Everyone is already seated when I walk into the dining room. Of course Grandma is going to put us in the formal room instead of us sitting at the table in the kitchen. I don't know how I'll last another second much less the rest of dinner. My blood feels jumpy with nervousness. My chest is tight with fear.

Silence lasts all of one bite of Grandma's delicious chicken and pastry before my mom startles me with, "What the hell is going on?"

My prim and proper mother just cussed.

"I...I don't know what you mean," I sputter.

"Marie said y'all were spending your days with some guy in a coma at the hospital you don't even know."

"I do know him," I lie. "Grandma and I both do. Marie failed to mention that I actually met Isaiah last time I was here." This tidbit I thought of when I was unable to nap. "When I heard what happened to him, I was only being a good friend by checking in on him. He hasn't had any visitors, so we've been visiting him." That's my nice little lie package.

"We think you should come home," Dad gently says. That's enough proof that he doesn't believe me.

Mom sends a quick glare his way. "You will come home, Chloe. You need to transition your focus to school and—"

"No."

Mom continues as if I never spoke at all. "Get ready to finish your last year of school. Then, you'll need to think about—"

"No!" I shout. The room immediately falls silent. "I'm not coming home," I blurt out, surprising even myself with my declaration.

"Excuse me?" my mom asks in almost a gasp.

"What about school?" Dad adds in a rush.

"What about Cody?" Mom asks.

Saying I wasn't going home was a huge step. Now they want all of my decisions up front? Gah. And now Mom wants me back with Cody? I bet he does look appealing to her when the alternative is me here in North Carolina. I've done such a good job moving forward; the last thing I need is for Mom to throw him back in my face. Hearing his name now makes me falter for a moment.

A shiver suddenly runs along my spine and I swear I hear Isaiah whisper in my ear, "Chloe, you can do this. What do you want? Just tell them what you want. Fight for *you* and no one else." If I didn't know better, I'd think Isaiah was standing right behind me this very second.

"I quit school and you know Cody and I are over."

Swear on my life, Mom clutches her pearls.

"I don't want to teach." Her grip tightens. "I want to stay here with Grandma and think about what I actually want to do with my life." There. I said it.

"Unacceptable!"

"She can make her own life's choices," Grandma interrupts my mom's impending unraveling. "I believe your father and I made no fuss when you wanted to up and leave with a man you had only known for three weeks."

My eyes bulge. I've never heard this part of my parents' love story. It seems so unlike my mom to do anything rash like that. She's always a person with a list and a plan and she always needs approval from society. What Grandma just said does not fall under that at all.

"Mother!"

It's a little funny to see my mom flustered like this.

"If this is what she wants, then you stay out of her way." Grandma looks at me, reaches over, and pats my hand. "You're more than welcome to stay here, sweet girl. Looks like y'all came all this way for a little ol' conversation."

"No," Mom protests. "This is not over. She is coming home with us."

Grandma taps my hand again and I realize she's said all she will to defend me at this point. She wants me to fight for myself some more.

"I'm twenty-two, Mom," I force myself to say while staring at my plate. "You can't order me to do anything. It's my life and it's well past time I make my own decisions." Deafening silence fills the room once more. Braving a peek, I stun myself when I glance up and catch the smallest of smirks on my daddy's face. That makes two people proud of me. Well, three, including Isaiah. "This is what I'm doing."

And that's where I exit the conversation. Mom continues on, but she's the only one talking and she may be the only one listening, too. All I want is to finish my dinner and get some rest. I'm tired. Plus, I'm anxious to see if I'll meet with Isaiah tonight. I can only pray that I do.

15

ISAIAH

"Isaiah?"

I look over my shoulder to see a worried Chloe. She rushes over and kneels in front of me, her hands on my thighs.

"What's the matter?"

"I am feeling weak today. I'll be fine." I hope. Cupping her face, I examine her. Something is different. "How are you?"

Her smile is brilliant. "I'm great, but we can talk about that later. Where's our bed?" Her brows pinch and then her cheeks flush as what she says hits her. I bet she can transform our bench, but she hasn't ever tried.

The bed soon appears and Chloe lies beside me.

"Why are you weak?" she whispers.

"Not sure, but I'm tired. Tell me what happened with you." The less we focus on me, the better. I don't want to talk about how I'm feeling. I'm worried enough as it is. If she has good news, then I certainly want to hear it.

"My parents came and I told them I was quitting school and staying here with Grandma."

Wow. Chloe did it. A smile lifts on my face before I can stop myself. "Good for you. I'm happy for you. You feel good about it, too, right?"

She nods. "Partly scared to death and partly like this boulder has been lifted off my chest." Chloe pauses, glances down, and then back to me. "You...you didn't...you didn't already know?" she asks with a great deal of hesitation.

"How would I?" I reply, confused. My day has been spent waiting to see Chloe, feeling tired and anxious.

"No reason." But now she avoids looking at me altogether.

"What aren't you telling me?" My voice remains gentle yet curious because her own anxiety is palpable.

"I could've sworn you were there, Isaiah," she begins with amazement in her tone. "I was so nervous and scared and second guessing everything, but then I heard your voice and the courage came back to me."

"Glad I could be of help." Not sure what else to say. As far as I know I wasn't there, but today has been weird and it's been hard to stay awake. "What are your plans now?" I ask.

"Figure my life out," she replies with a little laugh. "Wait for you." She watches me carefully for a reaction.

I smile. "It won't be much longer." That much I know in my bones. Whatever happens will be happening soon. Just like Daniel said.

"I'm grateful to have met you," Chloe whispers. Her eyes stare at mine with such intensity. "I don't think I would have been able to make these changes had I not." Her gaze drops to my mouth.

"You would have done it one day." I truly believe so.

"I'm thankful anyway." She smiles at me and I return her smile.

Chloe scoots closer and rests her head on my chest. We lie like that for a few minutes in silence. It's nice to be like this.

Certainly never thought I'd want to wake up from a coma because of a woman. It sounds so insane.

Chloe lifts her head, her mouth slightly parted as if she wants to say something, but then she closes it again. Her words of gratitude, as unusual as they seem to me, bounce around in my head. My hand gently wraps the side of her neck. I tug to pull her an inch closer. She doesn't resist. She doesn't yank away from me. Instead, her breathing hitches. With another tug, her lips rest against mine. Again, I wait for a reaction.

She seals her lips over mine. Kissing isn't new to me. But this kiss makes all the other ones feel like mistakes and insufficient experiences. This kiss is alive. We kiss each other as if our lives depend on it. Our bodies move in sync and a bliss I've never felt before bursts in my chest. This feels like home. Chloe, the kiss, it all makes me want more. More from life. More from and for myself. More for her.

It's terrifying.

I've never wanted that much more in life. I do what I need to get by and a little extra since I've been sober so I can get my brother back. What am I supposed to do with this?

All I can manage to do right now is continue to kiss her. Pulling away is as scary as continuing. But then…

"Chloe, wait." My eyes squeeze closed as a terrible thought hits me. "We don't even know what this place is or if…"

"If you'll remember," she finishes for me.

I nod. "Our first kiss should be in the world we know."

"I'm sorry."

"Do not apologize. I'm glad we did still, but this ain't the place." I can't help but look over at the hourglass. The end is finally near. Any day now the final grains of sand should run out.

"Is it weird that I think I'm going to miss coming here?" Her voice is soft and unsure. "I almost hope that once you're awake we'll be able to continue somehow."

"It is peaceful most of the time, isn't it? I think I may miss it too." I sigh because I can't believe I just said that. I roll toward her, away from the hourglass and take a deep breath. "Let's get some sleep."

She snuggles into me and I relax. There is so much weighing on my shoulders, but right now? After a kiss like that? I'm as relaxed as I've been since my parents died. I didn't know such a thing was possible.

"I'm grateful for you too," I whisper to Chloe once her breathing evens out and I feel as if she's asleep. I might have lost my mind or given up by now if not for her.

16

I wake up due to a loud knock on my door. As I roll over to face the door, my mother takes a step into my room. Before I can help myself, I groan. Her lips purse and her eyes narrow.

"May I come in?"

"It's too early for this, Mom. And unless you're here to tell me that you accept my decision, there's nothing to talk about."

She makes her way further into my room until she sits on the edge of my bed, her back straight and rigid. "You have three days to change your mind. If you haven't, then you need to buy a plane ticket and come straight home to get your things. I want you out. If you're going to do this, then do it all the way."

Three days? But...my mind quickly does the math. If I do this, that means I'll be gone when Isaiah is supposed to wake up.

"If you don't come, we're selling all your stuff."

That's harsh, but I don't doubt her one bit. She'll do it out of spite if for no other reason. I can't believe this.

"Fine. I'll book my ticket tomorrow because I know I won't change my mind."

If she could huff and stomp her feet without looking absolutely ridiculous, I bet she would. Instead, Mom stands with a heavy sigh. She eyes me with pity. As if I'm making the biggest mistake of my life. While there's still this big pit of anxiety and general uneasiness, I'm certain this is the path I need to take. That feeling is enough for me to continue to push forward through the not-so-great feelings standing in my way.

I plop backward after she's gone for a moment of peace but it's short-lived. My father knocks softly and pokes his head in.

"May I come in?"

"Yeah." I sit back up, ready for round two.

Dad sits in the same place Mom did, but he has a little smile on his face. "I've been doing a lot of thinking since Marie called us with that crazy story. I was thinking a bit about your future before that." Dad cups my cheek. "Honey, do what you want. You haven't seemed happy, especially this last year, and I want you to be happy. It's hard for me not to be able to help you and guide you; that's all I've ever wanted to do. I'm sorry if we pushed you too much or ever made you feel less than your sister. Just be happy and find your way, Chloe. If staying here and rethinking your plans will make you happy, then you have my support. I'll work on your mom."

This weight I didn't realize I was holding slides off my shoulders as tears well in my eyes. "Really, Dad?" When he nods, I bolt forward to hug him. "Thank you. Thank you so much."

"You're welcome. And whatever you might need, you let me know."

I thank him again and enjoy the comfort of being in my dad's arms while I still can. Knowing I have his support means more than I know how to express.

"Go on and get yourself ready for the day. Breakfast will be ready in a few," Dad says. He kisses my forehead and leaves me be.

If Dad is on my side and willing to try and talk to Mom, that's over half my battle right there. Mom will be a lot more willing to listen to him than me. She'll be more reasonable with him too. Even though I'm moving forward with my newfound willingness to stand up for myself and do what makes me happy, I still want their approval. I don't know if that's a good thing or a bad thing.

My parents leave by noon, keeping their trip as short as my mom's temper. I spend the day with Isaiah and tell him about all that's happened. I tell him about how I'll have to head home soon, so he'll be prepared for my absence in case I don't see him in dreamland again. I can't help but watch Rita. Could I be a nurse? I'm still unsure.

I split my time between crocheting and looking into more ideas for possible career paths. We're running out of time with Isaiah and I'm running out of time to make a decision if I want to be back in school by the fall semester.

I can't do this anymore. I'm running away. Can I crash with you for a few days? It's Jeremiah.

MY HEART POUNDS like a thousand stampeding horses when I see the text from Isaiah's brother. I leave in two days to go home and pack my things. Isaiah is supposedly waking up or staying like he is in three days. Now this?

I save his number in my phone and text back.

Me: *Absolutely. Where are you? I'll come get you.*

"We have a situation," I slowly say, peeking over at Grandma. It's late in the evening, so we're at home now. "Isaiah's brother seems to be in a bad situation and wants to run away. He asked if he could crash with me and I said yes. I told him he could reach out if he needed help," I add in a rush. Words begin gushing from my mouth as if I'm preparing for a fight. "He's Isaiah's brother! We have to help him. We can't let him disappear when Isaiah should be waking up soon."

"Chloe!" Grandma raises her voice only slightly, but it's enough to silence me. "It's fine. If his situation is dire, we'll certainly help him until Isaiah can."

My phone buzzes with an address and one word.

Hurry.

I grab the keys to my grandma's car, wishing my own was here. Within a few minutes, I'm across town and spot Jeremiah with a duffel bag hanging from his shoulders. He backs up when I roll to a stop in front of him. His body prepared to bolt. I roll the window down.

"It's me, Chloe."

His muscles relax and he lunges for the passenger seat. "Let's go."

"Are you okay?"

"As okay as my brother," he snaps. "If I wasn't desperate, I wouldn't have asked."

Okay then. In silence, we ride back to my grandma's house. It's stuffy and uncomfortable. We don't know each other, except that small link that Isaiah makes between us. Anxiety over allowing a stranger to come stay with me and my elderly grandma blossoms. But I keep repeating in my head that Isaiah loves him and I promised to help.

"Just this way," I say softly once I park and we exit the car. Once we get inside, I get a good look at Jeremiah. And I gasp. "Do you need a doctor?" I ask, taking a step forward.

He raises a flat palm. "Leave me alone. Where can I sleep?"

He's hunched to the right, cradling his ribs. His face is badly battered, covered in fresh bruises and blood. His lip is busted and one of his eyes is nearly swollen shut.

"Chloe?" Grandma calls. Her voice scares the daylights out of Jeremiah. He scurries backward into the front door.

"It's just my grandma; I stay with her," I say to him. "We're back," I call back to her just as she walks into the living room.

"Heavens," she breathes upon seeing Jeremiah.

"He doesn't want a doctor," I tell her before she can ask.

"Will you both stop staring at me?" Upon Grandma entering, Jeremiah has lost a smidgen of the bite in his voice. Not much, but a little.

It's as if something washes over my grandma when he says that. "My name is Gloria; it's nice to meet you, Jeremiah. Let me show you around, so you can get settled." And just like that, she acts as if nothing is amiss. Has she gone crazy?

"Thank you," he mutters so softly that I almost miss it. Jeremiah weasels past me and follows my grandma.

Well, at least we know he's safe. Hopefully, I'll see Isaiah tonight and be able to tell him what's happened.

But I fall asleep and I dream of boogeymen under my bed, coming after me and a scared little boy who cowers in the corner. To dream again is disappointing, especially with a dream like that. It worries me that I didn't meet Isaiah, but at the same time, I hope it's a sign of him waking up soon.

After a shower and getting dressed, I hurry off to the kitchen to check on our guest and my grandma. Both sit at the table. Jeremiah has cleaned up since last night as well. Unfortunately, his injuries are highlighted now as well. I join them at the table and Grandma hands me a bowl of biscuits.

"Good morning, sweet girl. I was just telling Jeremiah here that we usually visit his brother during the day, but I thought it best if you go alone today. We'll stay here. Jeremiah thinks he should stay out of sight for as long as possible."

I nod because there doesn't seem to be room to argue. Jeremiah keeps his head bowed toward his plate. "How long have you two been up?"

"Longer than you," she replies.

Well. Okay. I guess I'm not part of the little pair they've created.

We eat in silence for a bit before Jeremiah looks up at me.

"Do you think Isaiah will be okay with this?"

I give him the only answer I can. "I told him I'd help you if you ever needed it and I know that made him feel better, so I can't imagine he would be upset."

He nods and that's all he says for the rest of breakfast. Grandma talks a lot. She manages to get a smile or chuckle out of him, but he doesn't say another word. Maybe he's uncomfortable or nervous or a combination of emotions. He certainly hasn't had it easy in life. If we can offer him a reprieve from that, then it's nice we can. I hope it lasts long enough for Isaiah to wake up and get the ball rolling again for getting his brother out of that hell hole.

JEREMIAH IS a quiet kid based on observations so far. I don't think he trusts us at all and he's waiting for the other shoe to drop. But things have been fine with him staying with us. I wish I could actually talk to Isaiah about it. We haven't met back up again. It's hard to decide if this is something to worry about or not, but I'm worrying anyway. I can't help it.

The next few days will be one massive upheaval in both of our lives. I can only hope the transition will be smooth. Something deep in my gut tells me it won't, though. Today, however, is the day I fly home to pack up my things. I'm not looking forward to it. Somehow, I'm more anxious than before. It will take too long for me to return. Too long to pack. It will simply take too long. I'm even leaving earlier than Mom's deadline, but with me driving my car back, I'll be on the road for days.

My plan is to move as fast as possible. My dad will pick me up from the airport. I'll go home and pack until my car is full. Then I'm heading home, driving until I'm tired. I'll get a little sleep and then repeat.

Lucky for me, Dad is happy to see me once I land. There's a sadness about him, probably because I'm moving away. He talks and talks, which means he's nervous. Dad is a babbler. The only thing I can guess that means is Mom won't be as welcoming when I arrive home.

Sucks for her.

I'm bracing myself for it and my plan will be to ignore her as much as possible.

Nothing could have prepared me for what she did, though.

When I walk into the house, I find my mom and my best friend, who I've sorely neglected while visiting my grandma. Leah rushes over and smothers me in a hug.

"You abandon me. I had to hear about your grandpa from your mom and then she tells me you're leaving!" she finishes with a gasp. "What has happened to you? What in the world are you thinking?"

I glare at my mom, who smirks. Grabbing Leah's hand, I say, "Come help me pack and we can catch up."

After I've dragged her up to my room, I close the door. My heart constricts as I'm hit with photos of Cody and me from a happier time hung all over the walls. I never had time to take them down. He's everywhere. He's been on my mind more than ever. Once again, it's been tempting to contact him, but we haven't spoken at all since our breakup.

"What's wrong?" Leah asks from behind me.

"Nothing." I move forward and begin searching for my suitcases while she plops onto my bed.

"So, you finally told them you hated going to school, huh? Your mom expects me to talk you out of all this, but I sense a juicy story, so let's hear it. I don't have long before I have to get back home to my ball and chain and the kids."

Leah is the same age as me, but she got pregnant right out of high school. I'm the only friend who stood by her even with her having a baby. The others fell off one by one. She works a full-time job and went to school at nights for radiology until she could get the job she has now. Her parents helped out a lot, but then she met Tim and they got married within a year. It didn't take long before she was pregnant again. She loves her life and always says she would never change anything about it.

"If I tell you the full truth, you'd never believe me."

Leah chuckles at that. "Is there a guy? Is he better than," her mouth forms a frown while her nose crinkles. "I'm sorry; I can't bring myself to actually say his name. You know who I'm talking about." She notices the pictures, stands, and starts taking them down for me. My heart pitter-patters at the sight, but I ignore it and laugh at her antics. She never liked Cody.

"Yes, there's a guy. I don't know if he's better than Cody, but he's pretty great. Between him and my grandma, they've helped me slowly and surely find my voice to speak up to my parents. So I made the decision to move away, take some time to rethink my life, and—"

"And fall in love along the way," Leah finishes.

"Hopefully," I agree softly. "Help me pack. I need to get back soon."

"Only if you tell me the full truth." She grabs a box my dad placed on my bed for things I want to put into storage and begins packing things she knows I won't want to take with me on this journey.

I begin to tell her the story about Isaiah, ignoring her disbelieving looks. It feels nice to have my friend back. She's a lot like Grandma, but much more outspoken. She can unnervingly read me. Sometimes, I feel as if she knows me better than I know myself.

She thinks I'm looney. She says as much. But she doesn't tell me I shouldn't go. She helps me pack. She helps me load my car. She stands by my side as my mother storms into my room when we grab the last of the boxes.

"You were supposed to make her stay!" she shouts.

Leah laughs. "Sorry. She's made up her mind. I really tried."

"Chloe, think about this. You're throwing away college. A career. Your family!"

All I can do is shrug. "If you say so. I have to do what's best for me, not you." That's my mantra right now. That is what's pushing me forward. "Excuse me." I sidestep her to leave my room and head back to North Carolina once and for all.

Dad waits for me by the car. As soon as I'm close enough to hear him, he starts lecturing me. "Once you get tired, go ahead and call me. I'll find you a nice hotel nearby to spend the night and it's on me." Mom won't like that. He takes my box and then the one from Leah. "You'll get back to your grandma and that boy soon enough, but there's no need to rush. Take your time. Promise?"

"Promise," I reply with a nod. Dad turns to face me with a gentle smile. He pulls me into his arms. "If you ever need anything, you can always call me."

"Thanks, Dad."

Leah wraps me in a tight hug as well, grants me well wishes, and then it's time.

For a moment, my feet are frozen in place. A massive sensation of pure and simple overwhelming emotion washes over me. I can do this, I remind myself. It's for me. It's for my life. This will make things better. It's a new, fresh start.

I repeat those things in my mind over and take the steps to move to the driver's seat. I can do this.

I will do this.

But first I have to make a stop at the gas station. After I pump gas, I decide to grab something to drink and some snacks. I load my arms up because it'll be a long drive.

"Chloe?"

I whirl around. My breath whooshes right out of my lungs. "Cody."

"Hey. I thought it was you." He gives me an easy smile and looks me over appreciatively. "Planning a big night?" he asks as he spots my snacks.

"Road trip." Why is it so hard to talk to him? Those two words are all I can manage.

"Oh? Alone?" He looks around, as if expecting to find someone else with me.

"I'm moving away." Cody's jaw drops in shock. "To North Carolina."

His brows pinch with hurt. "You weren't going to tell me?"

I shrug. The cashier calls me forward, dragging me back the real issue at hand: leaving town. Does Cody truly expect a heads-up that I'm leaving town? I mean, I may want to tell him, but I don't owe him that. He hasn't reached out to me since we broke up and despite the many times I've thought about it, I haven't contacted him either.

"What are you going to do there?" Cody asks as I check out.

I think back on my conversation with Leah and give him a partial answer. "Find myself." I grab my bags and turn to face him. "It was good to see you. Good luck with your career." I hurry past him before he has a chance to say anything else.

Being around my parents again and now Cody? It's too much. I feel as if I'm getting sucked right back to where I was. It's a constant struggle to remember what I'm fighting for and why. The weakest part of me wants to run back into all of their arms and beg for forgiveness. But that is not the plan.

I nearly run to my car. It is way past time to leave this town and this life behind.

I'VE BEEN DRIVING for what feels like a week. Currently, Grandma is keeping me company while I drive. Her tone is off and I'm worried. Isaiah should have woken today.

"What's wrong?" I ask her flat out.

"I don't know where to begin," she replies with a sigh.

"Is it Isaiah? Jeremiah?"

"It's both of them, dear."

"Start with Jeremiah." I'm not prepared to hear about Isaiah yet.

"He's gone back, sweet girl." There's a hitch in Grandma's voice. Oh goodness. This cannot be good. "Somehow, they figured out he was here and came and got him. It was ugly, Chloe. I've already reported them to CPS, so I'm hoping we'll get some help soon. He knows to reach out when he can."

Her news kills me. I don't know Jeremiah that well, but hearing this breaks my heart nonetheless. I pull over and squeeze my eyes closed. "What else?" I whisper.

"Before he left, he told me something." Grandma's breath is shaky. "He thinks his foster parents are the ones behind Isaiah's condition. Did Isaiah tell you his accident was right before he was supposed to find out if he would get Jeremiah back?"

A sick feeling wraps around me. "No." He told me, but no. Surely they wouldn't have done this.

"Well, he was. Jeremiah said he's heard some whispering lately and can just make out enough to know they are talking about Isaiah. That it seems like they know he's in the hospital. He knows they switched cars in that time. He thinks it's them and I don't know what to do with that information, I'll be honest."

Me either. I don't want that weight on my shoulders right now. Not when I'm so far away. "What about Isaiah?" He's been so far away from me since we last met.

"Nothing has changed."

"He hasn't woken up?"

"No, but he's been twitching his fingers and his hands. The nurses think he might wake up soon." She does her best to sound hopeful.

But if something was to happen, it should have by now.

"Thanks for calling, Grandma. I think I just want to be alone with my thoughts and drive for awhile."

"Okay, sweet girl. I'll call you again tomorrow."

"I'm hoping to be back tomorrow night," I remind her.

"Hurry on." She's told me to take my time every other time we've spoken. Her telling me to hurry means she's truly worried.

17

ISAIAH

W here the fuck is Chloe? She's supposed to be here! She told me she was staying. I can't feel her anywhere. She hasn't been to visit, not to the hospital or to our place. I can feel my body awakening and yet I'm still knocked the fuck out! What is going on? I don't even think Gloria has been by. It's hard to tell for sure. My mind is struggling to make sense of things because I can feel myself fighting to wake up, yet I can't.

I don't understand what's happening. With every minute that passes with me still in this stupid fucking state, the more pissed I get. The need to wake up is more alive than ever. It's as if every molecule but one is on board with waking up and because that one is refusing to cooperate, I'm at a standstill.

If I could pace, I would be.

My mind doesn't know whether to worry that something's happened to Chloe or be pissed as hell because she must've abandoned me. This is what happens when you trust someone.

No.

I don't know that for sure. Something could be wrong. Maybe she's dealing with stuff with her parents. Or maybe something happened to Gloria. I need to keep my cool until I find out for sure.

If I can ever wake the fuck up!

My frustration may be making things worse, but it's difficult not to be angry. I've wasted too much time as it is like this. I must wake up.

Footsteps walk with such purpose into my room. No. Not that person again. The strong odor of cigarettes jumps off of him or her and clings to my bedding for dear life. The slight wheeze every time they take an inhale rings throughout my room.

"That rotten brother of yours," she starts, sending ice through my veins. "He's starting to snoop around. The best thing for you both is for you to stay this way, or better yet die. He's ours now and forever."

My head shifts around.

"What are you doing?"

Suddenly, it stops.

"Fluffing his pillow while I check on him," she says.

Wait. Was she about to suffocate me with a pillow like they do in the movies? All she has to do at this point is pinch my nose! Jeremiah's evil foster mom scurries out of the room. This is even more proof that I must wake up and drag my brother out of there. I wasn't safe from them as someone who just wanted to care for him; he's certainly not safe in the house with them, especially if he's prowling around like she said he is.

This is the last thing I need on my plate right now. However, if I could wake up already, or meet with Chloe, maybe I can have her tell the cops about his foster parents.

Or if Autumn knew I was here, she could help me. She's my best friend, she'd definitely help.

Why the hell can't I wake up already?

Where is Chloe?

Maybe I need to sleep. Maybe then I'll go to our place, meet with Chloe, and figure out what's going on.

Sleep turns out to be just sleep. And that just pisses me off. Couldn't I at least go meet Daniel for him to give me some non-advice advice? I started seriously freaking out hours ago. All my life, I try so hard to remember the love my parents gave me, so I can give that to Jeremiah. I try to remember the easy trust I placed in people, so I can fight the mistrust that comes naturally to me now. I try to be open-minded instead of judging all the time, although I almost always fail.

But what's the point?

Where does it get me?

Absolutely fucking nowhere!

"Okay, Isaiah." Jeremiah's lowered voice brings me out of my inner rant. "I need some advice. I'm pretty sure Rosa is the one who hit you with her car. I really want to confront her, but maybe I should go to the police instead. But I don't know what to do if they don't believe me, or if Rosa finds out. They're already madder than hell that I ran off to Chloe's for a while. I just don't have anywhere to go if it goes sideways. And they keep talking about coming up here to finish the job. I don't want them to get that chance and actually do it either." He sighs. "What am I supposed to do?

Whether we like it or not, we both need to trust in the system for once. He needs to go to the cops.

"Shug." The sound of the nurse who I used to think was evil startles us both, I think. "If you know who did this, or think you know, you need to go tell the police. I'm sure he wouldn't mind."

There's a tense and uncomfortable silence.

"You know what? My shift ends in ten minutes. If you want, I'll drive you down there and hang around while you give your statement. How does that sound?"

The quiet of the room doesn't last as long this time.

"Sure. Uh, thanks."

"Stay right here and I'll come back as soon as I've clocked out."

Footsteps get softer as she leaves the room to Jeremiah and me. I hear him inhale. "Guess I'm telling the cops. I hope it's the right decision, Isaiah."

18

"Sweet girl, where are you?"

I groan. Huff. Sigh. I release air any way I can think of to show my frustration. "I'm stuck in Tennessee. Something happened with my car and I'm waiting for the part to come in so they can fix it. It's going to be another two days."

It's unbelievable all of the obstacles getting in my way right now. It almost makes a girl want to rethink her recent life decisions. But I'm not and I won't. My mind is still made up.

If the stars would only align so the process would go a little smoother. Then again, maybe this pit of anxiety in my stomach is performing some self-fulfilling prophecy voodoo.

All I want is to get settled and start my new chapter in life. Driving as much as I have means I've done entirely too much thinking. Three times I've been extremely tempted to turn around and drive home. More times than I care to admit I've slacked in the faith department that everything will work out as it should. Isaiah and I haven't met in our dreamland. The deadline has passed and he still hasn't woken up. Whether he stays like he is now or wakes and doesn't remember me battles for the number one stop under My Greatest Fear. I likely think of him more than I should. More than is healthy for sure.

But I've grown to care for Isaiah and I'm invested in what happens to him. If only **something** would actually happen!

"I'm sure you'll be back on the road in no time." Grandma's unwavering positivity brings me back to our phone conversation.

"I hope so," I grumble. "How's Isaiah?"

"No change. Still twitching. Jeremiah went to the police about his foster parents and it's opened a big ol' can of worms. They've moved him, so maybe this new home will be better for him." She pauses briefly. "Oh! Jeremiah ran into Isaiah's best friend. He was able to tell her what's been going on, so she was here today too."

Oh, great.

She has surfaced.

Those annoying pings of unwarranted jealousy rise within me again.

"Her name is Autumn. Peculiar girl. Doesn't say much. Very suspicious of me. I thought Jeremiah would be a hard nut to crack, but I'm afraid he has nothing on this girl."

Grandma's report of her doesn't help my feelings either.

"Well, I'm glad she knows now; Isaiah is probably happy about it too. I have to get some rest. I'll call tomorrow." It's been a long day and sleep sounds fantastic right now.

Sleep, however, has been a source of anxiety. I'm so ready to get home that I don't want to sleep, but I also want to sleep and hope I run into Isaiah. It doesn't help that my hotel room is big and empty. I've never stayed in a hotel room alone before this trip. It's such an odd feeling. It is liberating in a way too. I triple check that the door is as locked as can be, shower, and slip into the bed.

Please, please, please, Lord. Let me meet with Isaiah.

FINALLY.

I'm here in our dreamland. A cool mist kisses my ankles. A lavender scent fills the air this time. The temperature is that perfect not too warm, but almost too chilly air, as if fall is on its way. Our bench sits in its usual place. The view is the same as it normally is; a city skyline resting miles away, twinkling in the night sky.

But my heart stops as I realize two key things at once.

Isaiah is not here.

No more sand falls through the hourglass. In fact, the area around the hourglass is completely dark. It's five shades darker than the rest of the land. Shrouded in a gloomy haze, the large hourglass stands tall and ominous.

No!

Why am I here without him?

What could this mean?

Dark, looming clouds suddenly roll in as if it might rain.

A crack of lightning shatters the hourglass. An ear-piercing scream scratches my throat as the energy from the bolt throws me backward.

"Chloe!"

Twisting around, relief pours through me at the sight of Isaiah running toward me. He's here. He kneels next to me, immediately wrapping me in his arms. I've never felt safer or more at peace than in this moment. It's bewildering that someone else can make me feel this way. It's terrifying that I might lose it.

"Are you okay?" he asks, cupping my jaw and nudging gently to force me to look at him.

"I'm fine. So happy to see you."

He smiles, but then it falters. "Where have you been?" His eyes search mine as if the answer lies within their depths.

"I had to go home to get my things; I told you once my parents left. Don't you remember?"

Isaiah glances down, his eyebrows pinched and his eyes lost in a field of confusion. We sit in silence for a long moment before he finally shakes his head. "No," he replies softly. "I can't remember that at all."

"At least you're here," I tell him, hope blossoming in my voice. "I didn't know what it may mean for me to come and you not be here."

"When will you be back?" Anxiety and fear laces his tone.

"My car needed some unexpected repairs so I've been delayed, but I should be back in two days. How are you feeling?"

"Like I am literally waiting for a switch to flip so I can wake up. I can feel it in my bones that it'll happen, but for some reason, it's not. I don't understand it and it's pissing me off." His hands form fists with the subject change and I wonder if he realizes it. "I'm having trouble staying conscious too. Well, you know, like being present to listen to people. It's getting harder to do that. I keep falling asleep. Real sleep. This is the first time I've been here since I last saw you." His hand unclenches as he cups my cheek again. His lips flatten with displeasure. "I'm seriously worried, Chloe," he admits.

"Why? You just said you know you'll wake up."

"What if I'm wrong? What if I do and I don't remember you? Pre-coma Isaiah…" His voice trails off and his gaze averts. "I've grown a lot during this time, Chloe. I don't want to go back to who I was."

I give him the advice I wish I could take myself. "We should try not to worry about it until we know what'll happen; there's nothing we can do about it right now."

He nods and rests his forehead against mine. "I'm losing strength; I don't know how much longer I'll be here."

My heart struggles to beat steadily.

"Can I kiss you?" he asks.

I'm one hundred and ten percent okay with that. As soon as I begin to nod my consent, Isaiah closes the distance and kisses me. It's so bittersweet.

There's so much hope and happiness in this kiss, but there's also an element of fear that makes this kiss feel like goodbye. That breaks my heart. Isaiah deepens the kiss. He drags me on an emotional rollercoaster. At times, his kiss tells me everything is going to be okay. Then, there's nothing but worry and clinging to what's built between us.

One moment, I'm overwhelmed by it all.

The next, Isaiah disappears mid-kiss.

Big fat tears form and slide down my cheeks before I can truly process the totality of the moment. Returning to North Carolina is the right thing for me to do. I can feel it in my bones that it's going to be the start of something great.

But something tells me my start will be bumpier than I'd like.

19

W hen I finally make it to Grandma's, it's as if a weight is lifted from my shoulders. It's been a long, long journey. I leave everything in my car, not caring to drag it in at this late hour. Using my key, I ease the door open.

The delicious smell of chocolate chip cookies hits me at once. Man, I love my grandma. Then, I notice the light is on in the kitchen and can hear voices talking softly.

"Grandma?" I call out.

"In here, sweet girl," she replies.

I should've known she'd wait up for me even though I told her not to. When I enter the kitchen, I'm caught off guard by the presence of Jeremiah.

"Hey, y'all."

"Hey, have a seat," Grandma orders. She stands while I sit. I'm too tired to argue even if I'd wanted to. She drags her feet over to the fridge, pours a fresh glass of milk, and returns to the table, nudging the plate of fresh cookies toward me. "Have a few."

"Thanks." I glance at Jeremiah, wondering why exactly

he's here. It's not that I mind, but it's late and he's supposed to be with new foster parents. Has something bad happened already?

"Jeremiah wasn't feeling quite settled in his new home and asked if he could crash here tonight. They didn't mind and of course, I didn't either."

"How are they?"

Jeremiah shrugs. "Too soon to tell. It's weird and I didn't want to be there tonight. I thought I'd keep Mrs. Gloria company while she waited for you."

He's unusually relaxed and talkative tonight. I've never heard him say so much at once before.

"We were just talking about Isaiah. We're certain it'll be any day now," Grandma tells me.

"Are you looking forward to it?" I ask Jeremiah, though I know it's a dumb question.

He nods. "There's a lot to talk about with him."

Isn't that an understatement.

"How was the rest of your trip? Do we need to go get your things?" Grandma goes to stand, but I wave her off.

"I'll never make a trip like that again." At least not alone. "I'm glad to be back. We can get my things tomorrow. I'm certainly not doing it tonight as late as it is, and as tired as I feel."

"Why don't you hit the hay then and we'll talk tomorrow," she suggests.

I nod, finish off my milk, and bid them a good night. I'm more than ready to see Isaiah tomorrow. The only uncertainty that lies within me is if Autumn is there. There's no reason to be nervous about her presence, but I am all the same. Maybe I can ignore her and focus on everyone's one goal: waiting for Isaiah to wake up.

~

AFTER UNLOADING my car and having breakfast, the three of us head over to the hospital. It's not until I see a girl sitting by Isaiah's side that I realized how much I hoped she wouldn't be here. She's not what I expected. She's a lot to take in. Her hair is pitch black and long, flowing down the length of her back. Her eyes are brown and outlined in heavy, dark eyeliner with purple eyeshadow to match. Her lipstick has a hint of purple to it as well. For as scary as she looks with the bold makeup and the scowl, she's a beautiful girl.

"How do you know Isaiah?" she asks, glaring at me.

All this time I've been worried about meeting her and I didn't think of a cover story! I glance at my grandma and happen to see that Jeremiah is also interested in hearing this answer.

"I...I, ah, met him last year when I got a summer job; we worked together." It's a complete and total lie, but it's all I can think of.

Her eyes narrow further. "You worked on a hog farm with him?"

Shit! I internally gasp at my cussing. Why did that have to be Isaiah's job? We seriously need to learn more about one another. "Yes," I reply. "My grandfather thought it would be a good experience for me, considering I live in the suburbs back home." How is it so easy for me to lie? Is my eye twitching? I feel as if my eye should be twitching to give me away.

She purses her lips. "It's odd that he never mentioned you." She raises her eyebrow. "Maybe you weren't that memorable."

Okay, so she's also a little mean.

"What's your name again?" I ask, unable to help myself.

"Autumn," she bites. "I'm his best friend."

I nod. "Right. I remember Jeremiah telling me that."

She stares at me for an awkward moment before turning her attention to Isaiah. I guess we're done talking now.

Standing next to his bed, I take his hand in mine. Whether it's Isaiah or simple reflexes, it's comforting to have him immediately squeezing my hand. Even though it feels like everyone is watching me, I can't help but lean down to whisper into his ear.

"I'm back now. Whenever you want to break through and wake up is good with me."

The nurse walks in and looks surprised to see so many more people than usual. "I take a few days off and when I return, Isaiah has so many more visitors." She smiles. "I'm sure he's happy about that. However, I must shoo you all out. The doctor will be in soon for a thorough examination and then we'll be running some tests on him. It'll be an all-day affair."

Of course. The day I come back, I can't spend any time with him. I squeeze his hand before leaving the room.

"What would you like to do today?" Grandma asks, trailing after me.

"If you don't mind, I'd like to hang here."

She frowns, but nods. "Well, I'm going to take Jeremiah home and run some errands then. Text me when you're ready."

"I have to go too?" Jeremiah asks.

"Yes. Your foster parents called me this morning and requested I bring you home by eleven. You also have an appointment with the police; they have more questions for you."

He doesn't seem happy about the news, but nods.

Grandma reminds me to call her once again and then off they go. I get comfortable in the waiting room. Well, as comfortable as one can be in a waiting room. Thank goodness I brought my laptop with me. I need to figure out what I'm going to do with my life.

The hustle and bustle of the hospital catches my attention to start with, though. Nurses talk softly about patients. Concern is clearly evident in some of their tones, while others sound frustrated.

"Your story is complete bullshit," Autumn says, plopping into the seat next to me. "I had lunch with Isaiah plenty of times out on that hog farm and not once did I ever see you. How do you really know him? If you know him at all."

I'm sick of her doubting me, though I know it's warranted. I don't have another lie in me, though. Leaning toward her, in a low voice, I say, "I know that on the night responsible for all of this, he got into an argument with you because he relapsed. Isaiah said if anything ever happened to him, you wouldn't try looking for him because you'd be worried you'd find him dead instead. Still think I don't know him? I can go on."

Her face is carefully blank, but she looks away. She's really pissed now.

"This makes no sense."

"Neither does Isaiah being in this situation," I argue back. She folds her arms over her chest and continues to stare straight ahead. Feeling awfully brave, I ask, "Are you not leaving?"

"I will once I figure out if you're worth my time or not."

Well, okay then.

I open my laptop and head to the local community college's website. I want to review their programs first and then those for the university nearby.

After about twenty minutes, Autumn turns toward me. "Do you have some sort of secret relationship with Isaiah? A romantic one?"

I...I can't really answer that question either. In dreamland, sure. There's something there. But here? I can't say yes given the circumstances.

"Your lack of an answer is answer enough. I can't believe Isaiah wouldn't tell me he was involved with someone."

"He had nothing to tell." At the time they last spoke, that was true enough.

She's quiet for maybe five seconds. "I still don't like you." Before the words that I don't like her either can leave my mouth, she stands and leaves. I guess I'm not worth her time. That's absolutely fine by me.

All day, I try to really focus on the various programs I can choose from, but I find myself getting distracted and caught in the rigamarole of the hospital. It's such an interesting environment. Giving in to my nosiness, I stand to walk around.

There are doctors, of course, but there are a lot of nurses. They run in and out of rooms. They talk sweetly to some patients, sternly to others, joke to some. Some nurses look tired, holding onto a cup of coffee like their own lives depend on it. Some look like they could go all day and are willing to fight anyone who gets in their way.

I wonder what it would be like to have their job. Almost immediately, I doubt that I could handle it. My thoughts turn to my grandparents. How could a person ever have the strength to watch someone die and be around when they hear the news? There's no way I have the guts for that. But maybe there's something nurse-adjacent I could do.

Once I return to the waiting room closest to Isaiah's room, I begin my search once more. There has to be something I'd have the guts for. By the end of the day, I've looked at a few different paths and feel as if I'll have a decision soon.

"You're still here?"

I glance up at the sound of the nurse's voice.

"Yeah. Is he back in his room? How is he?"

"Yes. So far, it looks like he's healed quite well. The doctor seems to think we're just waiting on him at this point."

Of course we are. Isaiah would be frustrated to hear that because he so desperately wants to wake up.

"Thank you for the news. Can I ask you something personal?"

Confusion causes her eyes to squint. "Such as?"

"How do you do this job? Especially when someone is like Isaiah and doesn't wake up, or is like my grandpa and dies."

The lady sits down next to me with a shrug. "It can be hard, but I also witness the amazing strength patients and their families manage to have to get through these hard times. Plus, there are some folks who have no family. All they have are the nurses who tend to them. There are a lot of hard, difficult days, but there's something each day that makes it worth every last hardship."

"Thank you."

She gives me a smile and leaves.

"The police interviewed me again today," Jeremiah says. "Pretty sure they agree with my suspicions, but they wouldn't tell me anything. Maybe we'll have good news by the time you wake up."

He falls silent. I struggle to stay and listen to him.

"I'm in a new place." His voice lowers. "They are new to the whole foster parent thing. Not sure if that's good or bad. I'm only the second kid they've gotten. They haven't said much about the first kid." He's quiet for a while again. "I don't think Autumn likes Chloe."

If I could laugh, I would. Autumn doesn't like anyone.

"She doesn't even seem to like Mrs. Gloria, which is crazy. Even I really like Mrs. Gloria." His tone drops again. "Sometimes, I wish I could stay with her until you're better. She's the nicest person I've ever met. Seems too good to be true," he finishes with a mumble.

"Anyway, I should go. Irene, the new lady I'm staying with, is waiting for me in the parking lot. I told her I wouldn't be long. I just wanted to tell you—"

Darkness swoops in and drags me away before I can

hear the rest of what Jeremiah wants to say. If I don't wake up and get the hell out of this hospital soon, I'm going to lose my mind.

"SHE KNOWS THINGS, yet you never mentioned her. What the hell, Isaiah?" I can tell, just by the way she's speaking, that she is talking to herself and not really to me. "How are we supposed to be best friends if you're keeping secrets?" Autumn makes some kind of sound. I may not be able to adequately describe it, but I know she's displeased. "She's so not your type either. She looks like a goody two shoes wrapped in a bow with a halo hanging over her head. It makes me want to puke." After a moment, she says, "How you really know her and your relationship with her is something weird. And gross. I'm sure of it."

I wish I could chuckle and shake my head at her.

"Or maybe you're oblivious to her evil plans because of the naivety she seems to have, but really, she's an evil mastermind and she's the reason you relapsed in the first place!" Her tone ends on such a note that it's clear Autumn thinks she's figured Chloe out.

This is not good. Chloe needs Autumn to think she's my friend and a good person. Otherwise, she's going to have a hard time on her hands until I wake up. One of the things Autumn was pissed about was who would've given me the drugs. Everyone we knew from our drug days knew I was clean. Autumn had threatened their very lives that if either of us ever returned begging and they sold to us, she'd mutilate a particular body part they hold dear. Some have ended up in jail. Some have died from overdoses. There aren't many left, but there was one who isn't scared of her. He's the one I went to and he's the one who hooked me up.

Unfortunately, she now thinks Chloe is up to no good. If only I could tell her that isn't true.

"Autumn. You're here early," Chloe comments.

Autumn, unsurprisingly, doesn't reply. Chloe takes my hand and I can feel my own hand react to hers.

"You aren't welcome here," Autumn finally says. "Not if you know Isaiah how I think you know him."

"You'd never guess how I know him. You know he can hear you, don't you?"

"That's fucking insane."

"Believe what you want, but I doubt he'd be happy with you telling me to leave. Besides, I'm not going anywhere. I've been here with him while you were too scared to even look for him."

Autumn releases a string of curses under her breath. "For you to look like a teacher's pet, you sure can be a bitch." Footsteps hurry out of the room.

"I'm sorry," Chloe whispers. "She's not nice to me and this weird backbone has appeared in my body that spews things out to her." She's quiet for a moment. "Maybe I should go check on her. Then again, I'm probably the last person she'd want to see." That is true. Chloe is better off leaving Autumn to steam by herself.

"I know you're probably frustrated, but just relax. It'll happen in due time, I promise."

"They arrested them!" Jeremiah shouts. His footsteps sound as if he's jogging his way further into the room. "The police found the car and some more evidence. They arrested both of them today!"

"Oh, that's good news, Jeremiah. I'm so happy for you

both. And I know you must be happy that they are out of your life for good."

"Only if they get convicted will I believe that," he tells her.

"It'll happen."

"Isaiah will be so relieved to hear about this once he wakes up."

"Yes, he will," Chloe agrees.

I'm already relieved and happy about it. I just need to wake the fuck up. Life continues to move on without me and I'm sick of it.

21

CHLOE

It's been two weeks. Two weeks of living in North Carolina. I've gotten settled into my room at Grandma's. I've been looking and applying for jobs to have a source of income. Every day, I endure time with Autumn for Isaiah's sake. Every day, I grow more and more concerned. I have not felt Isaiah's presence since Jeremiah's previous foster parents were arrested. He slipped away so subtly while Jeremiah and I were talking that I almost missed it. He's been gone ever since.

Today feels different, however.

My heart pounds in my chest. I stand next to Isaiah's bed, holding his hand. Grandma sits in the chair behind me. Jeremiah sits in the chair on the other side. Standing next to him is Autumn, who increasingly speaks less and less and, with looks alone, shows more and more distaste for me. Every chance she gets, she glares at me. We're all here, waiting for Isaiah to wake up as usual.

If it wasn't for Grandma telling stories from her life, I don't know that any of us could bear the uncomfortableness and awkwardness of the situation.

She's in the middle of telling us about one of the many Valentine's Days she spent with my grandfather when Isaiah releases a small groan.

Those seated immediately stand. We all hold our breath. We watch with amazement as his eyes flutter open. My thoughts hyperventilate.

This.

Is.

It.

He's.

Oh god.

He's.

Waking.

Up!

My heartbeat accelerates to a speed that must be dangerous. It's finally happening. It's really truly, finally happening. I hold my breath. Isaiah blinks and searches the ceiling with clear confusion. Autumn runs out to alert the nurses that he's awake. The movement of Autumn drags his attention to that side of the room. His smile is slow and weak.

"Jeremiah," he rasps. "It's good to see you." His brows pinch together. "What's going on?"

I still completely. He doesn't remember? *No.*

"You don't remember?" Jeremiah asks.

His face blanches. "The last thing I remember was storming out on Autumn and walking down the street. I don't remember anything after that."

No. No. This can't be happening. If he doesn't remember us meeting, then I'm a complete stranger. I have no place here. There is no friendship. No kiss. We have no history if he doesn't remember. I'm no one to him. God, please, *no.*

Isaiah turns his head to me. Those blank green eyes stab my heart. "Who are you?"

I squeeze my eyes closed. The day we've been waiting for has arrived. I'm thrilled for Isaiah and devastated for myself. There's no way I can explain myself and not sound like a lunatic.

With those three words, he's destroyed me. There it is. My worst fear. Confirmation that it's over. One knife slices straight through my heart.

"That's Chloe," Jeremiah answers. "She's a friend of yours."

"No," Isaiah replies slowly, trying to shake his head. "She's not." He continues to stare at me. It's almost as if he's trying to place me, but there's nowhere in his memory for me to be. "I have no idea who she is. I've never met her."

Knife two pierces my sternum. Tears fall from the corners of my eyes.

"But," Jeremiah starts to protest for me.

I shift my gaze to Jeremiah, needing a distraction. "It's okay, Jeremiah. It's more complex than you know. I should go. I'm glad you have your brother back."

"Chloe," Grandma starts, but I shake my head and rush out of the room.

My lungs pulsate as if I'm getting electrocuted. A small part of me now realizes I moved here for him. I disregard that stupid move. Trying not to focus on the devastation weighing down my entire body, I keep thinking, "*At least he's awake.*"

But that's the end of us. How do you introduce yourself to someone when you've told the people he loves that you already know him? How do you remind him of your time together when it was in a place that doesn't actually exist? How do you convince him he knows you when he doesn't? Not really. I can't even insert myself into his life. There's no way to do it without looking as fucking crazy as our situation is.

"Chloe!"

I blink and look up to find my grandma sitting next to me. Looks like I dropped myself in a waiting room chair.

"I'm so sorry."

Another set of three words that break me. I fall over into her arms and burst into tears.

"We'll figure something out," she reassures me. I don't know how we'll do that, though. The way I see it, my tie to Isaiah was just severed.

22

ISAIAH

Something nags at me while I'm being examined. When I told that girl, Chloe, I didn't know her, it was as if I could feel her heart breaking in two. As if I could feel how I poured gasoline over her hopes and then threw a match on them. It doesn't make any sense. Her palpable feelings were overwhelming. Relief and disappointment met me when she left the room.

Jeremiah hurries back into the room as soon as the nurses are finished. "What the hell, man?"

"You're already mad at me?" I question.

"How do you not remember Chloe?"

"He what?" Autumn chimes in. "I knew something was fishy! She might have known things, but something was up."

My eyes bounce between them. "I don't know her," I repeat.

"She knew about Earl, Isaiah. You are the only other person alive who knows about Earl. You know her." He's so adamant about it.

If she knows about Earl, though, then I'm confused.

How does she know that? If I do indeed know her, then why do I not remember her and only her?

I push those thoughts aside. "Will someone explain what happened to me?"

Jeremiah falls silent and takes a seat, deciding to focus on the TV. The last thing I remember is getting high, arguing with Autumn, and then going for a walk.

"The people the state deemed capable of looking after your brother didn't want you to get custody. They hit you with their car before you could try and get him back," Autumn says as casually as if she's reading a menu to me.

I was hit by a car? Driven by Jeremiah's foster parents? She goes into more details, such as how long I've been in the hospital. Jeremiah fills in that thanks to Chloe, who found him, he was able to find out what happened to me. He ran into Autumn one day and that's how she found out. I still don't know how this Chloe chick connects with me, but it sounds like she looked after me during all of this.

"You really upset Chloe," Jeremiah says, bringing her up again.

"Why do you care about her so much?" Autumn snaps at him.

"Unlike you, they've helped me," he snaps back.

"Maybe I should go back to sleep for a few more months," I try to joke. They fall silent and glare at me instead. "Do we know when I get out of here?"

"Not as soon as you'd like, I'm sure," Autumn answers.

She's right about that. I know I may have just woken up, but I'm exhausted from all the activity. "I'm takin' a nap." Autumn seems slightly alarmed at that, but I don't rightly care.

THIS DREAM IS ODD. It's full of déjà vu. I feel myself changing the environment to resemble a fairground, but then focus on this enormous Ferris wheel.

"Come on," I say to Chloe. What is she even doing here? I take Chloe's hand and we walk up creaky metal steps until we can take a seat on a red bench that will carry us up and around. Once we're buckled in, I look over at Chloe. "Ready?" I ask.

She nods. With a screech that makes me want to cringe, the ride begins to creep forward. It's nice to give this to her. Our conversation from earlier was a bit heavy; maybe this will lighten things up.

But then she surprises the hell out of me.

"I'm going to school for a degree I don't want."

I raise a brow at her.

"My sister went to school to become a doctor. She's the…" Chloe hesitates, but then continues, "she's the pride of the family and can do no wrong." I doubt that. Her parents must be proud of her as well. "Growing up, any time I voiced my opinion about something, I was always wrong or silly for thinking what I did. Soon, I just realized having no opinion was easier. Then I'd never be wrong. Never get in trouble. They'd always be happy."

"But?" I ask, sensing there is more.

"But my parents still aren't happy with me. I'm going to school to follow in their footsteps and somehow it's still not enough." She shrugs. "I'm making myself miserable for nothing."

We're at the top of the ride and it slows to a stop. The view around us expands to a nearby city, lit up with twinkling lights in the night sky. This is a view she loves for some reason and I gave it to her. A weird sense of pride builds within me and gives me the strength to give advice when I have no right to do so.

"You gotta buckle up, Chloe," I tell her. "There's only one person livin' your life and that's you. Live it for you and be miserable with your own choices but don't be miserable 'cause you're following someone else's direction."

I AWAKEN WITH A START. What the fuck kind of dream was that?

23

I get a job working retail. In general, people are nice, but there are some rude folks too. It's a job and it helps me pass the time. I work to think about my future and avoid thinking about Isaiah. I haven't returned to the hospital since he woke up. Although I want to, I don't see the point. Jeremiah comes to visit every few days, though. He gives updates on Isaiah. He's been released from the hospital. The police are disappointed that he doesn't remember more, and while they have enough to continue with their case, they still hope that he'll remember more details from that night.

Leah has tried calling me a few times, but I ignore her calls. I decline calls from my parents too. My focus is the reason I came here. To get away from my parents and take control of my own life. I've decided on a program to start in the fall. Sonography intrigues me and I can picture myself doing it. I've already started applying for the program, which is more rigorous than I was prepared for. Some days, I feel like I've already started school. I can only hope that I make the cut and get accepted into the program.

My career path is coming together. There's still the issue with my parents. There's still growing up and evolving I must do. But the relief I feel at knowing that the next time I step foot in a classroom, it won't be to obtain a teaching degree? Well, that feels amazing. Already the weight that rests on my shoulders is lighter.

Grandma pokes her head into my room. I didn't realize she was still awake.

"If you don't stop ignoring your parents, they are going to drive me up a wall. Talk to one of them for my sake, please."

"Yes, ma'am," I promise.

She smiles at me. "Thank you."

Tomorrow is Saturday and my parents have something else in mind to get my attention. During breakfast, there's a knock on the door. Grandma is pleasantly surprised to see Marie, but I'm disappointed. I wish she had never moved here, but she fell in love with North Carolina on our trips here much like I did. When she got a job opportunity here, she jumped on it. Now, she lives an hour away with a husband we only see at family events, and sometimes not even then. Apparently, he's a super busy guy and can't always make the time.

Whatever.

"Mom and Dad wanted me to check in on y'all."

"Glad you did, but I have to get to work."

Marie glares at me as if I just put a damper on her plans. I smile sweetly and decide I'm not interested in finishing my breakfast. Since I really do have to work today, I might as well get ready for my shift. Maybe I can manage to pull a double and completely ruin Marie's plans.

The day is steady enough. Part of me wonders if I should be fighting for whatever it was we had, but it seems impossible to do that when Isaiah doesn't know who I am. I don't even know how I'd convince him to get to know me all over again.

I step away from my post at the cash register for a quick bathroom break. My co-worker is around here somewhere, stocking shelves. When I return, though, I stop short.

Isaiah stands on the other side of the counter, waiting rather patiently for someone to check him out.

"Sorry," I softly say, closing the distance between us.

He stares at me with that intense gaze. For a moment, it's easy to get lost in the depths of his eyes. I look away, however. My gaze focuses solely on the items he's haphazardly dropped onto the counter. It's a bunch of snacks and a few drinks. Nothing out of the ordinary. There's so much I want to say to him, but I don't know what to say at the same time. It's really nice to see him upright and walking around, though.

Maybe he's piecing his life back together.

I reach for the last item, a candy bar.

Isaiah's hand reaches out in a flash and grabs my wrist. His touch is nothing like in dreamland. The sensation is overwhelming. It's a simple hand with calluses on the fingers. A simple hand that's warm and rough. But there is nothing simple about the way it feels. About how my heart thumps so loud in my chest, it's all I can hear. My knees weaken, even as his grip tightens.

"Look at me," he snaps in a low voice. He sounds angry. I've certainly never heard that tone before.

Reluctantly, I glance up.

"How the fuck do I know you?"

I swallow hard at the fury in his eyes. Why is he so pissed? My mouth opens, but a croak of a sound escapes as if my voice has gone into hiding as well.

"Jeremiah insists I know you." His voice drops even lower. "I keep having these weird fucking dreams about you and," his eyes squint in confusion, "my gut tells me I do know you, but I'll be damned if I know how."

He's having dreams? Hope blossoms. Maybe he's remembering our time in dreamland.

The bell over the door rings out and breaks the weird moment between us.

"Isaiah, what's taking you so long?"

We look over and my heart falls at the sight of Autumn.

"Oh. You," she snarls.

I scan the candy bar and spit out his total. The sooner they are gone, the better. Well, for Autumn at least. The tension is thick as we wait for Isaiah to pay with his card and for the machine to do its thing. Autumn grabs the bags. The only thing left for me to do is hand over the receipt and he doesn't wait for it.

A whoosh of air flies out of my mouth the moment they both walk out of the door. Regret hits me hard in the chest. I should have said more. Asked him to stay and speak with me. Or maybe we could meet up later. Autumn ruined whatever itty bitty amount of confidence I had, though.

The rest of the day is uneventful. Marie is sitting on the couch when I walk in the door of Grandma's home.

"You're still here."

"Yep. Just sit down and let me get this over with."

I sigh and sit in Grandpa's favorite recliner.

"Mom's off the rails about your decision to move here. But Grandma seems to think you're making the best decision for you." Marie huffs and leans her head back to look up at the ceiling. "I know we haven't been the best of siblings, but honestly? I couldn't see you teaching either."

My eyes widen at hearing this.

"Grandma said you chose sonography?" She lifts her head to look at me once more. When I nod, she says, "That's a cool field. You'll probably like it."

"What's happened to you?" I blurt out.

She ignores me at first. "Tell her what you want to do. She'll be happy that it's in the medical field like me and get off your back for a bit. If you need any help, let me know." She pauses for a moment and then says, "I wish we had a better relationship than we do, but I think Mom always got in the way of that. After spending the day with Grandma and hearing her talk about you, it's made me think of my own life and all the ways Mom influenced me. Maybe I need to be more like you and voice my opinions too."

She leans forward with her elbows resting on her knees. "Chloe, I have a husband at home and a hard job. I worked too long yesterday to be doing what Mom wants me to do, especially when it's an hour away, but here I am. I get what you're going through. It didn't hit me until today that Mom is the reason I'm a doctor. She dropped hints for me long before I realized that's what I wanted to do. She just happened to pick something I actually want to do. We're more alike than you think."

I'm having a hard time believing some of this, but she's so sincere. More sincere than she's ever been with me.

"I have your back," she adds.

"Thanks." I don't know what else to say. Maybe she's right. Maybe we are more alike than I thought. Did Mom really treat her the same as me and I just never saw it? There is a little bit of an age gap between us.

Marie stands and walks over to me, causing me to stand as well. She hugs me. Marie and I haven't hugged since...I don't even remember how long it's been.

"I'm going to visit more often. It'll allow us to catch up

,and I need to see Grandma more often anyway. Don't worry about Mom; I'll handle it. You take care of yourself." She waits until I nod and then moves on to find Grandma and say her goodbyes to her as well.

First, I run into Isaiah. Then, Marie turns all nice on me. This has been the weirdest day.

24

ISAIAH

I rock on my heels as I wait for Chloe to return to our place. The ground seems to rumble for a brief second before a blood-curdling scream shatters the air. I look up and my heart begins to beat into overtime as I see Chloe falling toward me. Dear God, what is happening? Fear like I've never felt before locks me in place, paralyzing me.

Closer and closer she comes. No. This can't happen. She can't get hurt. I can't bear the thought of it.

"Chloe!" I shout, as if that will accomplish anything.

With an oomph, I manage to catch her, falling to the ground in the process.

"Are you okay?" I immediately ask, pushing her hair away from her face so I can get a good look at her and try to see for myself in case I don't trust her answer. But she can't answer me. She only nods. That worries me more. "What the hell was that?" I demand to know. We can not risk her getting hurt. Chloe shakes her head. She's without answers. "Are you sure you're okay?" I ask, softening my voice.

The sound of glass cracking distracts us. That damn hourglass! I despise it so much. More sand falls out of the hourglass.

Chloe hides her face in my neck and I instinctively try to soothe her. I don't like seeing her stressed. "It's okay. We'll figure it out."

Chloe lifts her head. She's beautiful, even when freaked out. All I want to do is in this moment is make things better for her. But then I notice her blushing and I can't help but smile.

DAMN IT! I'm so sick of these dreams. They feel so real. The emotions are palpable. It's annoying and frustrating. I don't understand it. Nearly every time I fall asleep, I dream of her. Then there was that incident earlier today. The deer in the headlights look Chloe wore when she saw me haunts me all day. I still have this weird connection with her. She was so nervous to see me. When I grabbed her hand, she very nearly froze and it was as if she might faint. I could even tell she was relieved when I left.

Jeremiah is still pissed at me. Just because this girl somehow knew about Earl the Squirrel, he's adamant I knew her.

But. I. Don't!

Right?

I have no fucking clue about how she knows about the squirrel either. My dreams so far haven't clued me in. But just because I'm dreaming about her doesn't mean I know her, right? Dreams are dreams. They aren't events that have actually happened. Yet my gut keeps screaming at me that I do in fact know her. None of this makes any fucking sense.

Man, I wish I could get high right now.

But I can't and I won't because I shouldn't. It's been rough since getting out of the hospital. My position at work has been filled by someone else. My apartment has been leased to someone else; thankfully I didn't have much in it. I have nothing.

It pisses me off.

I worked so hard and for what? To get hit by a car, lose everything I have, and wake up to start all over again?

Autumn is letting me crash at her place, but I don't want to be there for long. Even though my brother seems to like his new set of foster parents, our goals haven't changed.

"Will you stop moping?"

I snap my head up at the sound of Autumn's voice. "I'm not moping."

"Is this about Chloe?" She fakes a gag as she says her name. "She's bad news, Isaiah. She was probably the one who sold to you that night and that's why you don't remember her."

I snort a laugh. She's not, but it's hilarious Autumn could even think so. "You've seen her, haven't you? I doubt she's even had a drop of alcohol, much less laid her eyes on drugs." She's so beautiful, though. That pisses me off too.

"Well, she's a weirdo from the west coast. There's no way you really know her. She brainwashed Jeremiah."

That's right. She's not even from here. How could I possibly know her?

But I do.

Somehow I do.

"I'M SERIOUSLY WORRIED, CHLOE," I hear myself saying. Worry floods my veins. There is so much on my plate. Admitting that I'm worried feels wrong, but I know that I can tell her.

"Why? You just said you know you'll wake up."

"What if I'm wrong? What if I do and I don't remember you?

Pre-coma Isaiah..." I look over to the hourglass. Pre-coma Isaiah is an asshole, even on his good days. I'm rough around the edges and not always good in social situations, even normal ones. I don't think pre-coma Isaiah would mesh well with Chloe. "I've grown a lot during this time, Chloe. I don't want to go back to who I was."

"We should try not to worry about it until we know what'll happen; there's nothing we can do about it right now." She sounds so sweet and I can hear the hope in her voice that everything will turn out just fine.

I nod and rest my forehead against hers. "I'm losing strength; I don't know how much longer I'll be here."

She exhales a shaky breath. With so much uncertainty before us, I want to take advantage of the time we have now. Of what is certain for us here before everything changes and possibly falls apart.

"Can I kiss you?" I ask.

As soon as she nods, I rush forward to kiss her. Something tells me this will be the last time I will get the chance. I deepen the kiss, needing her closer and the kiss to last longer. Maybe it'll be okay. But if it's not, then I need this moment to last forever.

I JOLT upright as goosebumps sprinkle themselves all over my skin. The dreams feel so real. But they also feel almost like a memory replaying itself. I don't understand any of it. Maybe I need to talk to Chloe again. The dreams are driving me insane.

But I also need to get a job and find a place to live. That's certainly more important, isn't it?

My phone rings with a call from my father. I've avoided them long enough, I guess.

"Hello," I answer.

"Oh, so you'll answer calls from your father," Mom snaps, clearly unhappy that I answered the phone when it came from his number.

I sigh. "What do you want, Mom?"

She's quiet for a moment. "I'm calling a truce," she bites out, clearly not happy about doing so. "You somehow managed to get your father and your sister to turn against me. Just explain everything to me, Chloe, and I'll listen without comment."

Something tells me she's going to have to mute her phone in order to get through whatever I say without comment. "Fine." If she wants to hash things out, then we'll hash them out. "You've never been supportive of me. You don't trust me to make my own decisions. I guess I reached my breaking point. I hated the thought of finishing my last year of school because it would put me one step closer to a life I didn't want. It was time I figured things out for myself, so I have."

"Sonography?" she questions.

"Yes. I think I'll like it. I've got a job here to have some money instead of relying on Grandma. I'll be back in school soon enough."

Things are quiet, but I refuse to speak next. It's her turn. "I never thought you incapable, Chloe." I snort at that statement. "I haven't," she insists. "It's just that you've always been so quiet and meek; we thought you needed as much help and guidance as we could give you."

So she thought because I was a quiet kid, I was a weak, dependent kid. That's even worse.

"Look, Chloe, when I left home to marry your father I was terrified. It was the only time in my life I didn't plan to do something. It's been well worth it, but it was also so hard for a while. Maybe that's because we didn't plan like I normally would have. You've never had a plan, Chloe. I guess I also thought I needed to build a plan for you."

"Well, I can make my own plans. I don't need your help." That sounds harsh, but I don't know how else to get it through to her.

"Okay. Will you at least consider moving back home?" She sounds so hopeful.

Mom misses me? That was something I honestly wasn't expecting.

"I don't want to," I admit. "I like being here with Grandma and I love Lupine Grove. I'm not going home."

Mom sighs. "Okay. I don't know how this happened where both of my girls moved away from me." She sounds so sad that I almost tell her I'll come back home.

But I stop myself before I can utter those words. This distance between Mom and me is a good thing. Like the coward I am, the distance helps me be brave. Mom and I continue to talk for another hour. It's actually pretty nice; nicer than I ever thought it could be. My relationship with her might very well improve.

That night, I fall asleep, wishing more than anything I could return to dreamland and meet the Isaiah I knew there.

～

No dreams for me.

Sunday is my day off. Grandma has invited Jeremiah over for lunch. I like that he's found comfort in visiting with her, because that's who he truly visits with, but it's a little awkward for me as well.

"Chloe, will you go into the attic and grab that box labeled Letters for me?"

"Sure."

I really don't want to because of the heat up there, but I'm not about to tell her no either. I wonder what the letters hold and why she wants me to get them. When I climb into the attic, it's hotter than the last time I was up here. It's harder to breathe already. Panting and sweating, I search for the box. Grandma only said it was labeled. There are a lot of boxes up here, though.

By the time I spot the box, I've been lightheaded for five minutes. I have to sit down when I find it. While I need to get out of here, my energy is depleted. I place the box in my lap and try to recharge my batteries, but black spots begin to overtake my vision.

Oh, no.

～

I GLANCE AROUND OUR PLACE. Any evidence of the hourglass ever being here is gone. A shout startles me and I look up to see Isaiah falling from the sky. Lucky for him, he lands on the bed. He rolls over and looks around, bewildered.

"Chloe?"

All I can do is nod. I'm not sure what mood Isaiah will be in or what this encounter will be like with him.

"Is this a dream?"

I shake my head.

He frowns and slides off the bed. He stalks over to me. "What the hell is happening?"

"This is how we met."

Isaiah throws his hands up in the air. "That makes no sense!"

"I know, but it's true. I'm not sure if you'll remember this or not since you didn't remember the other times we came here. My grandpa died, introduced us, and when we fall asleep, we come here." I shrug. "That's how I know you."

He folds his arms over his chest and rocks on his heels. "Do you know how crazy you sound?"

"Yep."

"So all those dreams were real," he mutters to himself. Isaiah shakes his head as if he can't believe it. "Those feelings?" He sounds so bewildered with himself. Isaiah looks at me, searching for answers. His eyes suddenly widen as he rushes toward me. "Why are you fading? Chloe? Chloe!"

I glance down at myself, but I don't get a chance to answer.

"CHLOE!"

I open my eyes to see Jeremiah hovering over me.

"Oh, thank goodness. Come on. Let's get you out of here."

With my grandma's box tight against my chest, Jeremiah helps me walk over to the ladder. My grandma stands at the bottom, wringing her hands. She looks so relieved to see me.

"You passed out on us, sweet girl. Thank goodness Jeremiah was here or I'd have had to call an ambulance."

It's all embarrassing.

"I have your box," I reply weakly.

"Just drop it down and get down here."

I do as she says. Grandma doesn't even wait for Jeremiah to come down from the attic before she's escorting me to the kitchen to sit. She puts food and a glass of water in front of me within seconds.

"I'm fine, Grandma," I reassure her.

She completely ignores me.

"Are you okay?" Jeremiah asks, entering the room.

"Fine. Overheated, I guess."

He sits down at the table and pulls his phone out, looking a little confused. I eat some of the food Grandma has given me because she keeps glaring at me. She'll start shoveling some in my mouth like I'm a baby here soon.

"What's in those letters?" I ask.

They must be important for her to send me into the attic of hell.

Grandma glances at Jeremiah. It's as if she isn't sure if she should tell me, which quite frankly annoys me a little. Jeremiah shrugs, but I can tell he's uncomfortable about her spilling the beans.

"He's having some trouble with his brother," she says with a nod toward our guest. "I wanted to show him something that may help him understand." Well, now I'm just confused.

"What do you mean? Understand what?"

"What it's like to live with addiction and how it affects others."

My brows pinch together. I'm still not comprehending in the least. How would Grandma know any of that?

Grandma chuckles, reaches over to rest a hand over mine, and says, "Sweet girl, why do you think we've never had any alcohol in this house?"

"Because you're Southern Christians and alcohol is the devil's poison?" I reply as if it should be that obvious.

Grandma laughs. Jeremiah even smiles. I'm as lost as ever. "Chloe, your grandpa battled with alcohol addiction for much of his life. He was a recovering alcoholic for forty years."

I blink. And I continue to stare at her blankly. This can't be true. It makes no sense. Not my grandpa. My brain and heart don't know how to process this. How could he never tell me? How could no one ever tell me?

"Honey," Grandma says gently. "He was a veteran," she reminds me. "He had a lot of demons he wrangled with, even to the day he died. We wrote letters back then and I was hoping Jeremiah might gain some insight into the struggle for both sides by reading our letters to one another. You can read them at another time." She slides the box over to Jeremiah. "You read them whenever you're ready, dear."

"Thanks," he says.

A loud banging on the front door interrupts us all. Feeling a little like a third wheel and needing a distraction, I offer to answer. Nothing could have prepared me for the person on the other side.

"Isaiah, what are you doing here? How do you know where I live?"

"Jeremiah told me. We need to talk." His hair is wild as if he just had a crazy dream, which I guess he did. He didn't bother fixing it before he rushed over here, though. His eyes are bloodshot and he can't stand still. "Chloe, I'm losing my mind and you're apparently the only one who knows what the fuck is happening. So, let me in and talk to me in a place that's normal!" he snaps.

"Isaiah?"

He jerks his attention to his brother who walks toward us. "What are you doing here?"

"Doesn't matter. What are you doing here?"

"None of your business, little brother."

There's a new tension between them that wasn't there before. I wonder what's happened. "Come on in, Isaiah." I step out of the way. "We'll go out back."

He nods and follows me through the house. Grandma says hello to him and Isaiah is polite in response, thankfully. For a moment, I was worried he wouldn't be. I lead him to a wooden swing, made more comfy with cushions, and take a seat. For a moment, he hesitates to sit next to me, rocking back and forth on his heels, but then he makes the decision to take his seat.

"Freaked out over meeting in dreamland today?"

He gaze snaps over to me. "That was real?"

I nod. "I think it only happened because I fainted. Seems one of us needs to have an issue like that for us to go there and meet."

He leans over to cradle his head in his hands, stopping us from rocking. "I don't need this bullshit on my plate too," he groans in a low, frustrated voice.

"What happened between you and Jeremiah?" I bravely ask.

"Autumn told him I was using that night, so he's pissed." Just as I wonder why his best friend would ever do such a thing, he continues, "I got into another argument with her the other day. She can be hateful." He shrugs his shoulders as if that's all there is to it. Isaiah takes a deep breath, leans back, and looks up at the sky. "Explain it all to me again."

"When my grandpa died, he came to me and brought you, saying you needed my help. He said that you were close to giving up and that I might be able to help you hold on. Grandpa even visited my grandma. We started meeting in that place when we were asleep, but not really asleep." How do I tell him about how we became friends and kissed and got really comfortable together? This Isaiah is a completely different person.

Isaiah waves me off. "I've had enough dreams to piece together the rest. Don't worry about telling me more; I can tell you're nervous about it." His voice is surprisingly gentler now.

"Am I that obvious?"

His body seems to release its tension as he gets comfortable, sitting much like I am, and begins to rock us slowly. "No. I just..." His pause lasts too long for my comfort. He glances over at me and shakes his head. "I can just seem to be able to sense what you're feeling. You can't with me?"

I shrug. "I don't know. You only seem angry so far."

Just like that day we spent at the beach, he laughs one of his *oh, that really tickled me pink* laughs. "That's true enough. Comin' outta this hasn't been as easy as I'd thought it'd be. It was only a few months and I lost everything." I expect another sigh, but he only gives me heavy, heavy silence.

So badly I want to ask if he needs any help, to offer him the same words I spoke to his brother, but I don't think it'd go over that well. Sorry doesn't seem to be the right word either. I don't know if he'll find any comfort in these words either, but here goes nothing.

"I promised I wouldn't go anywhere, so I'll be here if you need anything."

He pierces me with that gaze, making me realize how weird things are. Normally, it's hard to get out from under his gaze. "Thanks," is all he says. We stare at one another for a long moment and then he says, "Do you mind if I sit here for a while?"

"Not at all."

I stand to leave him be, but he grabs my wrist much like he did in the store. "You can stay."

Certainly didn't expect him to say that, but I'm not about to protest.

Chloe is still a little on edge, despite me telling her she can stay. To me, that's a peace offering. To her, I'm afraid it's more confusion. While my peace offering was genuine, I almost wish to yank it back. This is uncharted territory for me. Everything within me tells me she can be trusted, but I'm not trusting my own instinct on this one. It's too weird. And that's saying something after the apparent last few months I've had.

I fold my arms over my chest and squeeze my biceps.

"Do you really think I'm angry all the time?" I ask, knowing full well that I *am* angry all the time.

"You appear so," she says. "Are you saying you're not?"

"Not saying that." I wish I could say more, but I don't trust myself yet.

"You probably have a lot to be angry about," she says quietly.

I look over at her in surprise. No one has ever acknowledged my shitty life in that way. "Like what?" I ask, testing her. How much did I divulge when I was in that other place and clearly out of my mind?

Chloe looks away. She doesn't want to answer this.

My knee nudges hers. "Spill."

"Your parents died when you were young. Your brother puts a lot of pressure on you because he relies on you so much. You made a mistake with the drugs and now, you have to deal with that addiction. You get clean and have to deal with staying clean. There's a lot on your plate."

She knows entirely too much, just as I feared.

"This is fucking weird."

Chloe nods in agreement. She glances down. "I kept wishing when you woke up, you remembered. Part of me feels bad about it, but on the other hand, I don't know how to deal with you."

I laugh, which makes her crack a smile. She likes it when I laugh. Why I care, I don't know. "I don't know how to deal with you either."

Our silence after that is oddly comfortable. I wonder how long I can stay here. The only reason I asked to stay is because I have nowhere to go but Autumn's and I want to avoid going there. The only place I have to go is the only place I absolutely don't want to go. Her place is entirely hers. Having my own apartment, a place I could actually call mine, was so liberating and freeing. To have that taken away destroyed me more than I thought it would. It's going to take entirely too long before I can save the money to get a place to stay again.

"Isaiah," Chloe starts, a question clearly on the tip of her tongue. Her hands wring together and she glances back and forth between me and something just to the left of my head. She takes a deep breath and starts again. "Do you think we could be friends, Isaiah?"

I laugh. I can't help it. How was I ever friends with someone so...sweet? Chloe frowns, mistaking my laugh for me thinking her question is absurd. I immediately stop. Part of me wants to grab her hand. The act would comfort her. Her hand would feel familiar in mine. I know it would, even though I've never held her hand in what feels like a solid memory.

I don't dare take her hand, though. We aren't actually that friendly and familiar with one another.

"Yes," I reply. "I..." Damn, I'm insane. "I'm sorry for laughing." Since when do I apologize for something like that? "You caught me off guard. I don't see why we can't be friends, except..." I pause and grin as I realize she hangs onto my every word. This is fucking weird and amazing. "I don't have friends," I continue in a low voice, "and I don't like people."

Chloe laughs. "That doesn't surprise me. But I can teach you the ways of the world, Isaiah." But then she frowns. "Well, the tiny part that I know. I'm not that worldly. You're way more knowledgable than I am."

"Why do you say that?" While I dream of our time together, I still only remember bits and pieces once I'm awake and the memories fade with every waking moment.

She simply shakes her head, not wanting to delve into this topic further. That's fine. I certainly won't push. My hope is that if I give her space in times like this, she'll return the favor for me.

"What was I like?" I ask after a few minutes, wishing to view myself from her perspective.

Chloe smiles. Her gaze is off on a tree across the yard. "Still a little standoffish, but once we spent some time together, we began to trust one another. You were nice, protective, caring, flirty." Chloe's cheeks flush with her last description. "You'd change the scenery to give us something fun to experience."

None of that sounds like me. Then again, I've managed to sit here with her for nearly an hour.

"Where would we go?" I ask.

Her smile widens. "My favorite was the beach." Her smile fades. "Although it didn't end very well. We both were drawn out of the dreamland and woke up choking on salt-water." Chloe glances at me. "Well, you didn't get to wake up, but you were drowning on it. That was a scary night."

"Do you like the beach?" I don't want to talk about our time together anymore.

Chloe shrugs. "I've only been a few times. We don't live close enough to one back in Oregon and while we are close enough here, my grandparents never really cared to take me that often." She gives me the cutest sideways glance. "You?"

"Shouldn't you already know?"

She laughs, but waits for me to answer anyway.

"Yeah, I like the beach."

"How come you're hanging here?"

My frown is immediate. "Let's not talk about this anymore, Chloe. You'll ruin my good mood."

"You're in a good mood?"

My lips lift involuntarily at how she genuinely sounds surprised. I struggle not to laugh. This is bizarre. She's actually good company. "A mild one, but yes."

Chloe looks over at me with a smile. "I changed my mind."

"About what?" I ask curiously.

"I kind of like this Isaiah."

Why does that make me happy?

My phone buzzes with a text from Autumn. She's here to pick me up even though I haven't texted her to come get me yet. That's how much she dislikes Chloe.

"My ride's here," I say. Her disappointment rattles my

bones to the core. It's unsettling how much I feel her emotions. "What's your number?" She's surprised for only half a second before she spits it out to me. "I'll talk to you soon. Thanks for today."

Chloe only nods and stands. I smile at the thought of her walking me around front. I can tell when Chloe spots Autumn in the car. Overwhelming jealousy and annoyance war over the fact that she feels that emotion emits off of her. At least, emits from her and hits me. I grin. I like that she's jealous, though I shouldn't. Chloe rolls her eyes at me and pushes me toward the car, toward the very source of her jealousy.

"Don't you worry your pretty little face," I call out to her. It's impossible not to tease her. Surprisingly, I can't tell what her reaction is to it.

Isaiah is a little weasel. He spends the day with me, says we can be friends, and I haven't heard from him since. It's been two months. Jeremiah still comes over every so often, often frustrated over something, but he comes to see Grandma. I'm an outcast even here.

Summer isn't technically over, but it might as well be. I made it into the sonography program and have officially started that. Between school and work, I stay pretty busy. I do love North Carolina and staying with my grandma, though.

Life feels...scary without Isaiah. It's terrifying to think such a thing. I didn't realize how used I was to his presence until I had absolutely none of it. How much I craved him. How much I wanted him. Still I ache for him. Honestly, it pisses me off.

It's worse that he got my hopes up. He got my hopes up and then disappeared. It shouldn't sting as much as it does. Everything we had was basically fake. None of it was truly real, right? No matter how real it felt, it wasn't.

"Chloe?"

I glance over at Marcus. He looks frustrated. Can't say I blame him. Marcus was hired a few weeks ago; we manage to get quite a few shifts together and he's probably one of my first official friends here; Isaiah no longer counts.

"Have you been listening to me at all?"

"Sorry," I reply with a shake of my head. "What did you say?"

A concerned look crosses his face. "Are you okay?"

"Yeah," I say with a little bit of a sigh.

Marcus sidles up next to me, leaning against the counter. He's the polar opposite of Isaiah. He's friendly and carefree. "You need to have some fun. Maybe get laid."

With a glare from me, he holds his hands up in surrender. He's also a bit forward. The first day we worked together, I was cranky. Very, very cranky. One of the first things Marcus said to me was, "Damn, girl. Just get laid already." That pissed me off even more. He still thinks it's funny to say.

The bell jingles, drawing our attention to the door. The air in my lungs stalls. There he is. His eyes find mine immediately and he frowns at Marcus's proximity. He stands just inside the store, his arms folded over his chest. Isaiah rocks on his heels.

"Can I help you with something?" Marcus asks.

Isaiah doesn't look at him once.

"Can we talk, Chloe?"

Marcus whistles. "Now I know why you're pissy," he mutters under his breath to me. Acting as if we're better friends than we are, he throws an arm over my shoulders. "And if she doesn't want to?" he asks Isaiah.

Isaiah's face hardens in seconds flat. He chooses to ignore him, though. His behavior is uncalled for, all things considered.

"I'm working."

He doesn't like my answer, but I don't care.

"You can take a break," Marcus says to me. He tries to speak in a low enough tone that Isaiah won't hear, but he stands five feet away.

"Chloe, please."

Marcus nudges me.

I huff, brush past them both, and walk outside. The air is still hot and humid. My shirt seems to stick to my back immediately. It's days like this that I miss home. If only for the weather. I walk down the length of the store to be away from it and any potential customers that may walk past.

"You seem pissed at me."

I whirl around to face Isaiah. I thought I was mad when my ex-boyfriend broke up with me, but no. That was akin to being pissed about someone cutting me off in traffic. At least, that's what it feels like in this moment compared to what I feel like right now. This is an emotion I have never truly encountered before. I want to ask him what happened, but maybe I don't want to know. Maybe I need to wash my hands of this crazy situation.

"Are you gonna talk to me?"

My mouth opens, but I close it again. Isaiah seems content to wait for an answer, though, so finally I ask, "Why does it matter? You clearly don't care to talk to me."

"You don't know what's been happening in my life."

"I wonder why," I snap.

Isaiah's eyes widen in surprise and then he has the nerve to smile. "Trust issues, remember?"

I roll my eyes. "Nice job working on those."

His smile turns into a grin. "I don't remember you being this snarky. You were a lot nicer to me before."

"You don't remember much of anything. What do you want, Isaiah?"

"I remember more. I know I've sucked as a friend." At that, I scoff. "But I was hoping you'd give me a second chance. As much as I don't wanna be in this situation, I can't help but wanna be around you." That kind of sounds like he's been fighting what was between us and that's why I haven't heard from him. "You don't even know what it's doing to me to be here asking you for this."

Hearing that, I really truly look at him. Tension does seem to have his shoulders set in a slightly hunched position. His hands are holding onto his folded arms rather tightly. He's stressed the hell out.

"Are you okay?" He said I didn't know what's been happening in his life; what all has been going on?

Isaiah gives a quick shake of his head. His honesty surprises me. This Isaiah is more like the one I knew. "Will you meet with me?"

Without thinking about my decision, I nod.

Relief floods his body. He catches me completely off guard when he pulls me into a hug. "Life's been shit, Chloe," he whispers in my ear. "If I don't change something soon, I'm going to fall underwater again." Upon hearing that, I hold on tighter. The last thing Isaiah or Jeremiah needs is for Isaiah to relapse. "My gut says I've been wasting my time and I need to be around you, so that's what I'm gonna do if you'll let me."

"Whatever you need."

Isaiah releases me, appearing a bit flustered himself by his actions. "I'll be in touch. Promise."

My instinct is to doubt him, if only due to his recent behavior, but I can't deny something is different this time too. Isaiah forces a smile before walking away. The car he gets into is different than last time and there's no Autumn. Maybe he's been able to get a car already? That's good news.

"So?"

Marcus pokes his head out the door. We obviously need to be busier because he has too much time on his hands to be concerned with me and my life.

As I head inside, all I say is, "He asked for a second chance."

∾

Hey, it's me.

I SMILE when I see the text. It's been two days since I last saw him. My first thought is that it's Isaiah. But a girl can never be too sure.

Me: *Me who?*
Isaiah: *It's Isaiah.*

I fall back against my chair. He actually came through. My smile can't help itself.

"Don't let that phone distract you, sweet girl," Grandma orders as she spies me from the living room. "You have important homework to do."

"Yes ma'am," I reply seriously, even as I roll my eyes. "It's Isaiah, though," I can't help but add on.

"Oh. Carry on then."

A laugh escapes me. Even with whatever Jeremiah's frustrations have been lately, she stills roots for Isaiah. I hurry to respond to him.

Me: *Just checking; how are you?*

Isaiah: *Fine. U?*
Me: *Fine, just drowning in homework.*
Isaiah: *Do u want 2 go out 2moro?*

Whoa. He didn't waste any time at all. I'm supposed to work tomorrow, but Marcus doesn't. Maybe he'll switch shifts with me? My brain also wigs out at how he's shortcutting in his texts. Why can't he just spell all the words out? I take a deep breath and remind myself that this doesn't matter. I know he's a smart guy and he's a nice guy. It doesn't indicate anything except he's lazy when he texts.

Me: *Can I let you know in a bit? I'm supposed to work, but want to see if I can work something out.*
Isaiah: *K.*

Okay? No. Not okay. K. The letter makes me shudder. I don't know exactly the response I was looking for, but *K* wasn't exactly it. My phone vibrates in my hands with another text.

Isaiah: *We can meet after 2. Or another day. U don't have 2 go out of ur way.*

But I do. I want to more than I want to breathe. Doesn't he understand how long I've waited for this? It may seem like a short period of time in the grand scheme of life, but it feels like a chunk of my lifetime.

I text Marcus instead. If there's any love in the world at all, he'll fulfill this favor of mine. With bated breath, I continue with my homework, my gaze straying to my phone from time to time. If Marcus wants me to get laid so bad, then surely he'll come through for me. No. Not the right line of thought to have. I'm not getting laid! Isaiah only said something about talking and being friends. Nothing more. If that's all we'll ever be, that's disappointing. I'll still take that relationship from him, though.

My phone lights up. I snatch it as fast as I can to hopefully read the words I want to see.

Marcus: *You got it babe. Go get laid.*
Me: *Thank you so much!*

My fingers can't manage to get to Isaiah's conversation fast enough to text him.

Me: *Tomorrow it is.*
Isaiah: *K. Good. Pick u up at 6?*
Me: *See you then.*

I may have hoped that he'd continue to text me. My hopes may have been extremely high. Isaiah disappointed me. That was the last I text I got. Maybe he doesn't like texting? I wouldn't be opposed to a phone call. Is the only time we'll speak a few texts here and there, but primarily in person?

Chloe! Stop! You sound like an obsessed crazy person. Deep breaths. It'll progress how it'll progress. Besides, tomorrow is the day we've been waiting for. Finally some alone time with Isaiah that he's actually planning to do. Time with him that is in this realm. It'll be me and him at last.

What could go wrong?

"You're out of your fucking mind, Isaiah," Autumn grumbles, falling onto her couch, which has been my bed since I was discharged from the hospital. "I don't even like her. Why do you?"

She's been pissy ever since I told her I was seeing Chloe today. I hate to admit that she's been a big reason why it's taken me so long to reach out to Chloe. I've always been able to trust Autumn, even when I didn't think I could trust myself. When I wasn't feeling too sure about going with my gut, I relied on her and her word. Unfortunately, she despises Chloe. I think a large part of that boils down to the fact that Chloe is an outsider who wiggled her way in when I was vulnerable and Autumn wasn't there for me by her own choosing.

Now that I've gone against her advice? Well, she isn't taking that kindly.

"There's nothing wrong with Chloe except she's not from here." Of course, we Southerners like other Southerners best; I think it's in our DNA. But I have to admit that I like that Chloe didn't grow up here. She doesn't have our accent. She grew up in a damn suburb! We don't even have a true suburb that close to here. It's intriguing.

"There's a lot wrong with that girl. Not to mention how you say you met her is totally fucked in the head."

Yeah. I told her the truth about Daniel and our place. Autumn made me do an at-home drug test to see if I'd been using again; that's how off my rocker she thought I was. I almost think she was disappointed when it came back negative. She bounced back quick though and immediately asked me if I needed to be checked into the psych ward.

"What are y'all even going to do?" she asks, curiosity getting the best of her.

"We're going to the beach."

Autumn frowns. "At night? Why?"

I shake my head. She wouldn't understand why. "She'll like it; that's all that matters." Two things that stick out for me the most from when I was unconscious is our visit to the beach and that it was otherwise always night. I'm just combining the two. My statement to Autumn about her liking it is a lot more confident than I feel.

"What time will you be back?"

"Are you gonna wait up for me?" I tease.

"No," she snaps. "Are you bringing her back here?"

"No." Autumn's question implies sex. I'm not doing that with Chloe yet, especially when this ain't even my place. "Holler if you need me," I say on my way out. It's what we always say, even if she is mad right now.

Normally when I'm on my way to pick up a girl, it's just another day. Just another ride in the car.

Not today.

Today I'm nervous as hell. We're not even going on a date. At least, I don't think it's a date. It feels like one with this many nerves going nuts inside my body. As badly as I want to get high to make these feelings go away. My grip tightens on the steering wheel. No. I will not have those kinds of thoughts tonight. I've come too close to slipping too many times already. Tonight will not be another bad night of me jonesing for a high.

Tonight is about Chloe. Chloe with her non-Southern accent. Her easygoing smile. She's always willing to help. She's sweet. Sweeter than any girl I've ever met before. It's mind-blowing. My hands slowly relax their grip as I drive.

But when I pull up to Chloe's, my anxieties churn into overdrive. It pisses me off a little. She's only a girl. But as I was just thinking. She's not just a girl. A beautiful, sweet, smart girl. A girl I sort of know and trust, but don't really. At least, not when I think with my head instead of my heart.

With a deep breath, I get out of the car and walk slowly to the front door. Another deep breath and I know. Three hard raps to the solid wood.

Ms. Gloria answers with a large smile. "Isaiah. It's so nice to see you again. C'mon in. Chloe is almost done getting ready."

I follow her inside, smiling at the sight of her pink slippers. She shuffles her feet until she reaches the recliner. I take a seat on the couch.

"How have you been?" she asks. She picks up yarn and a needle, then she begins effortlessly working with it, her eyes on me.

"Okay. You?"

"Doing just fine and dandy."

Chloe breezes into the room. She looks slightly flustered. "I'm ready," she announces.

She wears blue jean shorts and a purple shirt with sandals. Simple. Cute. Perfect for where we're going. I relax even more because she's not overly dressed...as if this is a date. Chloe looks me over and relaxes as if thinking the same.

As I stand, she moves toward the door.

"I'll be back, Grandma."

"Never thought you wouldn't be, dear," she replies with a chuckle.

Chloe rolls her eyes at me, but I grin. She follows me out of the house and then we walk next to one another to my car. Her eyes widen slightly when I open the door for her.

"My, my," she whispers. "I really am in the South."

I chuckle and close the door behind her.

"So where are we going to talk?" she asks.

"You'll see."

She's quiet for a moment and then as if forcing herself to ask, she says, "How's Autumn?"

"Why do you two dislike one another so much?" It's slightly amusing to me.

"We got off on the wrong foot, I guess." Autumn often does that, so that makes sense to me. "I try not to feel the way I do about her, especially because I'm sure she's had difficult times too, but I can't seem to help myself. It's so out of character for me."

"I know that feeling," I grumble. To me, every reaction I have involving Chloe is out of character.

"How's Jeremiah?"

The subject change is nice, but unwelcome at the same time. When I glance at her and shrug, I catch a glare before I return my eyes to the road.

"How do you not know?" There's a bite in her voice that I didn't know she was capable of. "After all we've been through, after all *you two* have been through, why is your relationship a shrug?"

"I thought you didn't know how to speak your mind." I

hoped we'd have some peace on the beach before things turned too ugly. Chloe waits for an answer, refusing to acknowledge me until I answer her first. I sigh. "Do you have a sibling?" I think she does, but I can't remember for certain.

Her shoulders drop a tad. "Yes. An older sister. We don't always get along, but things are a little better right now."

"Well, it's different when you're the oldest. All the pressure is on you." I quickly look at her, hoping she truly gets it. "Especially when your parents are dead and he's relying on you. Add on that his foster parents tried to kill me and we keep having to deal with court mess, things are stressful. Jeremiah has these high expectations. High, Chloe. High as fucking Heaven itself. I'm a constant disappointment to him. So, yeah, things haven't been well when he's still in the system because my life isn't back together yet." My tone turned harsher right there at the end. Harsher than I intended.

The car is filled with a tense silence. At least it smells good, I guess. Pretty sure we have Chloe to thank for that. Her perfume fills my car, breathing life into it.

"I'm sorry," she finally says. "Jeremiah comes over a lot to see my grandma and I guess I just keep seeing this kid who was so relieved to hear you weren't dead. I wish you two didn't have such a hard time is all."

"Me too," I whisper. My relationship with my brother has always been a hard one. Nothing has changed. "How about we just listen to music until we get to where we're going? You can pick a station and then I will."

Chloe jumps at the chance to do so. It's nice to get to know her taste in music. It's vastly different than mine. My ears bleed from listening to her pop music, but she's a champ and listens to my rock music, so I don't say a word either. I think she's having a bit of fun with it because she doesn't even mention how long our drive is.

She perks up as we get closer to the island. I wait for her to say something about where we are, but she doesn't. Her hand grabs hold of a necklace she's wearing, though. Never noticed she was wearing one before. Does she normally wear it? Or did she put it on for a special occasion?

"The beach?" she whispers. "Oh, Isaiah."

That might be the best reaction ever. Hearing my name roll off her tongue like that? Damn, she could give me goosebumps. I find the beach access I frequent. Chloe hops out before I can cut the car off. Someone's excited.

I grab the bag from the backseat. It has a towel for her to sit on, just in case she'd rather not sit on the sand. There's a flashlight in there as well, in case it gets too dark before we leave. Even though Autumn might not've been happy about this, she was still a good friend. She helped me with a picnic-type setup, so I have food packed as well for dinner. We meet at the front of the car. I hold out my hand, which she takes. See? Another out of character thing for me to do. It seems simple, but it's not for me. Her hand is warm in mine. Soft. Smooth.

We make our way onto the beach. She is instantly mesmerized by the ocean. The crashing waves are as gentle as they are strong. The misty salty air dances along our skin. The air is a mix of that gross ocean smell that is obviously influenced by the fish in the sea, but it's also that heady scent of sunshine, salt water, and sand. It's as if I've brought a kid into their first mansion-sized candy store.

While she's focused on that, I decide she deserves the blanket, whether she wants it or not. I unfurl the towel and have a seat. Chloe glances back at me.

"But the water," she says as if she can't believe I've taken a seat already. I laugh and stand once more. She grabs my hand, slips off her shoes, forcing me to do the same, and drags me to the water. A shaky breath leaves her as the water rushes to cover her feet. "This is much better than dreamland and my memories. Thank you so much."

"Come on. Let's eat before it gets too late."

Her eyes light up and she follows me back to the towel. I have sandwiches, potato salad, chips, drinks, and some fruit. She seems happy with what I have to offer, which I'm thankful for.

"Tell me what's been going on with you," she says quietly as we begin to eat.

"Didn't I already? When I explained about Jeremiah?"

Chloe rolls her eyes, which makes me smile. "That was the short version."

"The best version."

"I thought you wanted to be my friend. Friends spill." She gives me a pointed look.

"Fine." But where do I start? Do I really have to? Whatever comes to mind first is how I'll go. "Autumn's pissy as usual. She's not happy about the Jeremiah situation either. She's worried I'll relapse. Jeremiah is pissed. His foster parents now are good, but that doesn't mean he's happy to be there. The jackasses who tried to kill me keep getting their court date continued out and the few things we do meet for is just simple bullshit; nothing that truly matters yet.

"I'm sleeping at Autumn's. Working again on a farm. Got this ride, but otherwise saving up to get my own place again. Every day, there is something that goes wrong, but every day, there is something that goes right too." She's staring at me like she understands. But also as if she doesn't understand why any of that prevented me from reaching out to her. "I don't do well with this shit, Chloe. You honestly seemed like something else to add to my plate and that was a hassle I didn't want."

She shocks the hell out of me when she nods in understanding. Why is she so easygoing? What is the catch? I don't understand.

"Catch me up with you." We don't need to talk about me any more right now.

Chloe launches in to tell me how she's mostly made up with her parents and her sister. She works at the store, which I already knew. She tells me which career path she chose. She sounds excited about her future. What I can remember of our conversations, that is a complete one-eighty. It's nice to hear. I wish I knew what I was doing with my future. Farm work is fine. It's good, hard, honest work. But I don't see myself retiring from it.

Darkness slowly falls.

"Shouldn't we be going?"

"No. You loved the night sky if I remember correctly. We're going to see some of it before we go."

She grins. Before I know what's happening, she scoots down and lies down on her back with her head resting on the towel. Now, she's all ready to view the night sky. She pats the space next to her. Clearly I'm to do the same. When a girl asks you to lie down, you do. No questions asked.

"I've missed this," she tells me once I'm lying next to her. "The night sky. You. Thank you, Isaiah."

"No problem. So what do you want in life, Chloe Romanski?"

Part of me expects her to have an answer immediately, but then I remember that she's had a hard time with this particular aspect. She's been doing well piecing her life together, though.

"I have the career part picked, so I'm happy about that. I guess, according to my grandma, I just need to find a man and settle down." I bark a laugh at that, causing her to laugh as well. "Some friends would be nice. I have one back home, and this guy at work, but I'm not sure if I want to count him."

Right. The guy who was super comfortable with her at her job. Not sure I like him.

Chloe props herself up on her elbow. She grins. "Jealous?"

"Not a chance."

"Uh-huh." She relaxes once more with her gaze on the sky. "This almost feels like us, Isaiah. I know you don't remember completely, but..." Her voice trails off.

"This was us, huh?"

"Kind of."

Not bad.

Chloe rolls onto her side, completely oblivious of the sand. "I kind of want to stick my feet in the water again."

"Well, let's do it." I sit up, but she doesn't follow suit.

"It's dark," she states plainly.

"So?" What difference does that make?

"It's creepy," she says as if it should be obvious to me.

I laugh. "I won't let anything bite you or drag you under," I say, standing. Although I've made this promise, and my hand is outstretched, waiting for her, she hesitates. A long moment passes before she grabs my hand and allows me to pull her up.

"I'm surprised it feels as nice as it does," she says as the water washes over our ankles.

Grabbing her hand, I pull us in further. The ocean has always amazed me. It can be calm and gentle, but there's always a deep almighty power, thrumming beneath the surface. You know that at any moment, she could suck you in and take you away forever if she so pleased.

"Too bad we can't go swimming," Chloe murmurs. We're almost mid-thigh on Chloe now.

"Says who?" I ask as I tug her close to me and launch us into an oncoming wave.

Chloe shrieks and sputters as she rises from the water, still managing to look like a goddess rising from an underwater kingdom. "Isaiah!" she hollers.

"Yes?" I reply with all the innocence I can muster.

She huffs, but she's smiling. "I don't have a change of clothes." Neither do I. This wasn't part of my plan.

"I'll treat you to ice cream on the way home to make up for it." That actually seems to make her happy. The water saturates our clothes and the breeze brings a chill to my skin. "C'mon. Let's get you dry." She follows me out of the water, standing by as I shake out our lone towel of as much sand as possible. "C'mere," I murmur.

Chloe inches closer to me and I wrap the towel around her shoulders. "What about you?"

"I'll air dry."

A lone eyebrow perks. Damn. She's too fucking cute. And sweet. Chloe tries to dry off so she can hand me the towel, but fuck that. I snatch it from her, wrap it over my shoulders, and hold my arms open.

"C'mere," I grumble, my voice huskier than I'd intended. But she's wet. Clothes sticking to her like a second skin. Hair hanging a little haphazardly around her shoulders.

With ease and no hesitation, she steps into me. This...this is amazing. My eyes close upon impact. I struggle to breathe when she rests her head on my shoulder. What the ever-loving hell is happening to me? On autopilot, my towel-covered hands run up and down her back in the name of drying off and nothing else.

Chloe looks up at me. "What all do you remember?" Her gaze drops to my mouth for half a second.

I know there was a kiss or two. I know I felt as if I'd lost my mind over them. But I don't remember them in crystal clear detail. Unfortunately, like most of my memories of our time together, it's fresh right after I wake up, but then it begins to get fuzzy.

"Not enough," I reply.

She seems disappointed. That simply won't do. My intent is clear as I slowly dip my head closer. She doesn't step back. She doesn't push me away. No. This beautiful girl lifts her chin ever so slightly as her eyes begin to flutter closed. That's all the sign I need.

Our lips meet. My arms try to crush Chloe to me, but I hold firm and tense to prevent them from doing that. She moans. That is nearly my undoing right there. I deepen the kiss even further. She grips my shirt in her hands. She presses her entire body against me. This kiss is slow, yet somehow frantic. If I could rip all her clothes off right this second, I would.

Chloe pulls away, stunning me. She looks as wild and overwhelmed as I feel. Her hair's a mess. Her lips are red and obviously freshly kissed. Her cheeks flush.

"I..." Her mouth clams closed. It opens, closes, opens again. "Maybe we should go."

She might as well have poured cold water over my head.

"Okay." I can't help but agree immediately. "Is everything okay?" She just did a one-eighty on me. I don't want to leave until I know for sure.

"It's getting late." True. "And that was overwhelming. You're too tempting."

I grin, causing her to laugh. I hand her the towel and pick up the rest of our things. We walk by moonlight to my car. It's been a good night. Better than I could've expected or hoped. We stop for ice cream as promised. We do the same game of finding good tunes and taking turns listening to them. It sucks when we finally arrive at her place.

"Thanks for a good night, Isaiah," Chloe says as I walk her to her door, wondering how we ended up here already. It's time to say goodbye. I don't want to yet.

"Want to do it again?" I hate the stupid nerves I feel with my question.

She opens the door, smiling over her shoulder at me, which means well for my answer. But she looks again and stops short at the sight of a guy sitting on the couch. I place a hand on her hip, just so she'll know I'm here if needed. Her grandma is where we left her, looking rather amused.

"Cody," she breathes. "What are you doing here?"

So she definitely knows him. The question is who the fuck is he?

"We need to talk," he says, standing. "Please, babe."

Babe?

Babe.

He said babe.

Chloe whirls to face me. Panic and confusion rolls off of her in waves. "Thank you," she says wholeheartedly. "I'm good from here."

That's as clear a sign as any that I should leave. My gut says I shouldn't. But I haven't been listening to it lately anyway. "Who is he?" I can't help but whisper.

"My ex." Sorrow at having to tell me this is evident. "We'll talk soon," she promises.

Mother fuck.

Shit.

Damn.

I knew my life simply couldn't accept anything good. Even Chloe has to come with fucking complications.

Two words.

Two words and she ruined out night, maybe even our future together. What in the world would I even do without Chloe?

THE END

Thanks for reading! The sequel will release November 12, 2020. Please consider leaving a review.

If you would like to hear news before anyone else, interact with Lindsay, and have a place to discuss her books with fellow fans, join Lindsay's League on Facebook. Be sure to sign up for her newsletter as well or visit her website.

ALSO BY LINDSAY PAIGE

The Hourglass Duet

Heaven and Hell Duet

Carolina Rebels series

Hearts in Carolina series

Sanity series

Bold as Love series

Bracing for Love series

Without a Doubt

Bending Under Pressure

You Before Me

Don't Panic

The Penalty Kill Trilogy

Oh Captain, My Captain series

The Ninth Inning series

ABOUT THE AUTHOR

Lindsay Paige is the author of multiple Young Adult, New Adult, and Sports romances. She also enjoys writing books with characters who deal with anxiety and depression, issues which are close to her heart. Lindsay is a North Carolinian who loves watching hockey, having conversations with her miniature Schnauzer, re-watching episodes of M*A*S*H, and living her dream of writing books for a living.

If you would like to hear news before anyone else, interact with Lindsay, and have a place to discuss her books with fellow fans, join Lindsay's League on Facebook. Be sure to sign up for her newsletter as well or visit her website.